Contents

This is for the love that thrives in the darkness, where hearts are bound by chaos and loyalty is paid in vengeance.

Content Warnings:

This story contains mature and potentially distressing themes, including:

- Exotic dancing and adult club entertainment
- Sex workers depicted within a club setting
- Sexual tension and highly explicit sexual content
- Sexual assault (non-graphic)
- Violence, including murder and revenge-driven killing
- Death
- Mentions of human trafficking and child trafficking (non-graphic)
- Pregnancy (announcement only, occurring at the end of the book)

Chapter 1

Maddox

Gunfire erupts in the night, a thunderous chaos slicing the air. I dive behind a rusted Buick, its once glossy paint now peeling, revealing patches of rough, bare metal beneath my back. The coolness of it seeps through my shirt, grounding me, even as bullets whiz past, ricocheting off nearby vehicles. My pulse races, each beat a countdown, but I force myself to breathe slowly, calming the adrenaline surging through my veins. I pop the clip from my pistol. Three rounds left. Shit. Not enough to waste a single shot.

The stench of burning oil, leaking gasoline, and fresh blood hangs thick in the air, but I shove it from my mind, focusing instead on the immediate danger. Edging to the car's bumper, I sneak a peek around it. Through the dense fog of gun smoke and dust, I spot him in the lamp post light, a fat guy barking orders, firing at my men with a manic grin. He's cocky and distracted. A perfect shot.

In a single fluid motion, I raise my weapon, aligning the sight with his broad chest. My finger tightens on the trigger. The gun bucks in my grip, and the shot punctures my target. His body jolts, and he crumples, hitting the pavement hard, dead before he even understands he's been hit. One less problem to worry about.

"Maddox." Jorge's voice breaks through the chaos, strained but alive. I flash a quick hand signal over the hood, just enough for him to catch it in the faint moonlight, if he's watching. I stay crouched, every muscle coiled. No sense in making myself an easy target.

The gunfire fades for a moment, replaced by an eerie, tense silence. I scan the lot, eyes darting over twisted metal and sprawled bodies. My men have taken down most of the opposing club's crew, bodies lying limp across the asphalt, patches of dark blood soaking into the dust. Only one shooter remains. He's pinned down, busy aiming at someone else, oblivious to me zeroing in on him.

I pull the trigger, and my final shot drops him instantly. His body slumps lifelessly, collapsing into a heap beside the car he'd taken cover behind. I stand up, holstering my empty gun, my boots crunching over shards of broken glass and twisted shell casings glittering like confetti in the dim light.

Geoffrey staggers over, clutching his shoulder, blood spreading across his torn shirt, but there's a fierce look in his eyes. He's hurt, but he'll live. We made it.

"Let's move," I bark, my tone cold, cutting through the silence as our adrenaline ebbs, replaced by the urgency of escape.

There's no time to waste. Sirens wail faintly in the distance, bouncing off the concrete, a reminder that we're on borrowed time. Ten minutes, if we're lucky, before the cops swarm in like vultures to sort through the remnants of our handiwork.

We make a swift retreat toward the truck stashed a few blocks away in a shadowed alley. It's not by accident that we chose this place. There's no CCTV or security here. Only a flicker of light from the streetlamps. Just darkness to mask our tracks. The truck is another piece of the plan, registered to Alan Hovack, a man who owes us a favor. We got his kid out of juvie, and in exchange, this mess will have his name tied to it, not ours. Whatever story he concocts for his van's presence won't involve us. It's a clean break, leaving the law chasing shadows.

I slide into the driver's seat, gripping the wheel. The tension simmers under my skin, that edge that comes after a job well done.

We're alive, still standing, still breathing. That's what counts after the bloodbath.

At the garage, the heavy scent of motor oil and grease envelops us as we pull in. This place is our cover, the front for our real work and the home base for the Zaffre Wolves Motorcycle Club. Geoffrey's arm hangs limp, blood seeping through his shirt, but he's one of the toughest men I know. The bullet tore through clean, no major arteries hit. We get him inside, patch him up, and he clenches his jaw against the pain, too damn stubborn to complain.

"Ey, Maddox!" Jorge calls out, his voice bouncing off the steel rafters above, breaking the silence as he tosses me a grin. "We hittin' the club tonight or what?"

I smirk, wiping Geoffrey's blood off my hands with a rag. "Damn right, we are. After today, I need a drink, and maybe something sweet to take the edge off." The buzz of the shootout still thrums in my veins, an undercurrent of dark satisfaction settling into my bones. Today, we ended the Copper Reds, a gang of parasites that had poisoned this town for years. They'd had it coming, every single one of them.

My father once ran this crew, kept us under the radar, cautious and careful. I'm not my father. I've been planning this for years, chipping away at the Reds, dismantling them piece by piece while they remained blind to the threat closing in. They didn't see the danger until it was already too late. Now they're nothing more than broken bodies on cold asphalt, the last of them gone before they could even name their killer.

It's not that I relish killing, but there are lines that shouldn't be crossed. The Copper Reds trafficked women, preyed on children, and sold human lives to the highest bidder. Scum like that don't deserve mercy. The Zaffre Wolves, we're not saints, but we have a code, a line we don't cross. By day, we're mechanics, fixing engines, passing as regular Joes. By night, we're something else entirely. A force that even the worst criminals fear.

The Wolves aren't just about protecting ourselves. We're the enforcers, the ones who step in when the law can't or won't. If you harm innocent people, we'll find you. When we do, we don't leave anyone standing. The media has dubbed us Avenging Angels, though our faces have never been shown.

As evening settles in, I slip into my usual attire, a pair of faded blue jeans that hug in all the right places, a snug gray tee stretched across my chest, and my worn, trusty Converse, still holding up despite how much

they have seen. It's time to let loose. The guys
and I fire up our bikes, the deep, throaty growl
of engines filling the night, slicing through the
quiet city streets as we head toward the Steel
Wings' gentleman club, Dancing Babes. The
wind rushes over my skin, crisp and biting,
cutting through the layers and leaving a cool
trail over the lingering heat from the day's
adrenaline. It's the kind of night where the air is
thick with possibility, each turn of the road like
a pulse under my grip.

When we pull up to Dancing Babes, neon
lights flicker in hazy reds and blues, casting
ghostly reflections on the pavement slicked
with the shine of city lights. The place is alive
with sound, the muffled bass pulsing through
the walls, drawing us in. Inside, the air is
heavy, wrapped in a heady mix of smoke,
musky cologne, and a perfume so sweet it
almost sticks to the skin. Bodies move to the
beat, lost in the low lights and the seductive
pull of the night. There's an unspoken promise
here, something raw and fleeting.

As the others break off, some slipping toward
the bar, others disappearing into private rooms,
I find myself at the counter, tossing back
whiskey that sears a path down my throat,
spreading a liquid warmth through my chest.
The burn takes the edge off, but I'm searching

for more than just the drink. Then I see someone I came here for. Raven hair spilling over her bare shoulders, fishnet stockings tracing every curve with precision, and a top that clings to her like a whisper, leaving little to the imagination. Her body sways to the music, each step a challenge, each glance a taunt.

Our eyes meet, and she smirks, her gaze dark and knowing. I know her well enough; she's familiar, reliable, but never boring. She moves through the room like she owns it, but tonight, I'm the one ready to take control. I cut her off, close enough to feel the heat radiating from her skin. "You up for some fun?" I ask, my voice low and rough.

Without a word, she curls her fingers into my shirt, yanking me closer, her breath warm against my neck. Her touch is electric, sending a jolt through me as her nails trail down my chest, her eyes holding mine, intense and unblinking. She leads me through the crowd, past a hulking bouncer, slipping into a narrow hallway where the noise fades, replaced by a thick, expectant silence. We enter a back room, the door snapping shut behind us.

The space is dim, lit by a single bulb casting soft shadows over her figure as she sinks into a firm cushioned chair, legs spread in a bold, unapologetic invitation. Her gaze is locked on me, daring with a smirk playing at her lips. Slowly, I drop to my knees between her legs, my hands tracing up her thighs, feeling the warmth of her skin beneath the mesh. My fingers hook under the straps of her thong, her scent wrapping around me, sweet and intoxicating, like a promise of escape.

"What's your rate tonight?" I ask, voice hoarse with need, hands sliding higher, gripping her hips as I pull her close enough to feel her pulse against my hands.

"Three hundred," she purrs, her nails raking lightly over my chest, leaving trails of heat in their wake. "And I'm yours as long as you want, baby."

"Deal." The words come out as a growl, my hands pressing into her skin, pulling her even closer. I breathe in the scent of her, my senses lost in the warmth of her skin, in the temporary oblivion she offers. For tonight, nothing else exists. Just the pulse, the heat, and the escape from everything waiting outside.

I yank her thong to the side and pull out my cock, hard and aching with need. With a swift thrust, I'm inside her, and her cry of pleasure echoes off the walls. The raw sound sends a shockwave through me. This isn't just about fucking, it's about reminding myself that I'm still alive, still human, even after everything I've done.

"Fuck," she gasps, her nails digging into my shoulders as I pound into her, my fingers working her clit, rough and relentless. Her body tightens around me, her moans growing louder with each thrust. "Yeah, baby, just like that," she pants, her voice breaking as she trembles under my hands, coming hard.

I flip us around, taking the chair for myself. She straddles me, lowering herself back down onto my cock, her heels digging into my thighs as she starts to ride. The way she moves tells me she knows what she's doing. She's done this a hundred times before. Shit, she's fucked me in ways that would have most people blushing.

"Fuck, you feel so good," I groan, thrusting up to meet her, my body straining to hold back. "Don't stop."

She leans in, her lips brushing my ear as she whispers, "You like that, baby? You like it when I take all of you?"

I grit my teeth, biting down hard as I try to hold on. "Yeah... What position you want tonight?" My voice is rough, barely more than a growl.

She smirks, her fingers sliding between us to rub her clit, teasing herself as she rides me. "On my knees. Face down, ass up."

Without hesitation, I grab her waist and flip her over, bending her over the arm of the chair with her knees perched on it nicely. Her face is buried in the cushion. She braces herself, and I don't waste a second. I slam back inside her, thrusting deep and hard, my body crashing into hers with each stroke.

"Fuck, you take this cock so well," I growl, my grip on her hips tightening as I lose myself in the rhythm. Her cries fill the room, her body arching under my touch, and I can feel her getting close again. "You want me to fill you up? You want me to give you so much cum that you'll leak all night long?"

"Yes," she gasps into the couch, her voice breathless. "Please, fill me. I want it all."

Her words send me spiraling. I pound into her harder, my cock swelling as I get closer, every thrust pushing us both toward the edge. "You're going to take it all," I growl, leaning over her, my breath hot against her back. "I'm going to come so deep inside you, you'll feel me for the rest of the night. No other fuck will replace the loss of me once I'm done with you."

Her only answer is a guttural moan, her body shaking as she comes again, harder this time, her pussy clenching around me like a vise. The sensation is too much. I explode inside her with a roar, my body trembling as I empty myself into her, the heat of my release flooding her.

When I pull out, I watch as my come drips from her, thick and slow, pooling between her legs. She's a mess, and the sight of it only makes me harder.

"So much," she murmurs, her voice hazy with satisfaction. She dips her fingers into the mess I've left on her thighs, bringing it to her lips before pushing the rest back inside herself.

She looks up at me, a lazy, satisfied smile on her face. "Was it worth every penny, baby?"

I give her a smirk, my body still thrumming from the release. "You're not done yet."

I sit back in the chair, watching as she stands before me, eyes dark with hunger as I make her turn around and face away from me. I grab her hips and slide back inside her, sinking deep into that tight, soaked pussy. It's raw, my cock still sensitive from the first round, but I don't fucking care. I need more. She moans as she lowers herself onto me again, bouncing wild and needy, her ass slamming down against my thighs.

"Fuck, yeah, ride me," I growl, my hand slipping between her legs to rub her clit. She gasps, her body tightening around me, trembling as I play with her, drawing out her pleasure.

"You like that, don't you?" I taunt, my voice a low rasp in her ear as I flick her clit in tight circles. "You're going to come again, baby. You don't stop until I say."

She tries to fight it, tries to squirm out of my hold, but I wrap my other arm around her waist, holding her close, forcing her to ride the orgasm as it crashes over her. Her moans fill the room, desperate and raw as she cries out, her body shaking uncontrollably.

"Fuck, you're squeezing me so tight," I groan, feeling her clench around me as she rides out the waves of pleasure. "You're not getting off my cock until I say so. You're mine for the night. No one else gets this pussy until I'm done filling it."

She's panting, her body trembling, but I don't let her stop. I rub her clit harder, making her whimper and squirm, her muscles spasming as I keep her locked in place, riding me until she's spent and my lap is coated in our release.

"Please," she gasps, trying to push my hand away, her voice hoarse from moaning.

"Nah, not yet. I paid for all of this. You're going to take every fucking inch until I'm done with you." I shove her off my cock, her body going limp from the intensity of the orgasm. I'm not finished.

I get her on her knees, grabbing a fistful of her hair, I guide her mouth to my cock, slick and hard. "Open up, baby," I order, pulling her head down onto me. Her lips wrap around me, her mouth warm and wet as she takes me deep. "Fuck, yeah. Suck that cock, slut."

I thrust into her throat, watching as her eyes water and her lips stretch around my girth. She takes all of me so good, letting me slide my whole cock into her mouth. "Take it all," I grunt, my fingers gripping her hair tighter. "You're going to swallow every fucking drop, you hear me?"

She nods, her throat tightening around my cock as I thrust into her mouth relentlessly. The wet sounds of her mouth working me echoes in the small room, her lips sliding up and down my length, her tongue swirling around my tip.

"Fuck, that's it. Just like that," I groan, feeling the tension coil in my spine again. "You're such a good little slut, aren't you? Love having your mouth full of my cock."

Her eyes meet mine, desperate and submissive as I push her head down further, fucking her throat harder until I can't hold back anymore. With a low growl, I explode, shooting deep into her mouth, my cock pulsing as I fill her throat with my cum. She swallows every drop, her throat working as I pump more into her.

"Fuck, baby," I groan, feeling her tongue working over me, milking the last drops of cum from my cock. "Every fucking drop."

When I finally pull out, I watch as a few more dribbles of cum slip from her lips, and she licks them up and swallows them without a word, wiping her mouth with the back of her hand.

"Good girl," I mutter, stroking my cock lightly, still not completely satisfied as I watch her stand up on shaky legs. She adjusts her soaked thong, tugging it back into place, then fixes her hair, pulling her top back down to cover her tits that had popped out, now flushed from the intensity.

I sit back in the chair, stroking my cock as I watch her, catching my breath. Then she collects her money and heads for the door. No cleanup, no conversation. Just gone, off to find the next guy.

I sit there, watching her leave, the high already fading, leaving behind the familiar emptiness. For a moment, I thought I'd escape it. As always, it's still there, waiting for me in the silence.

As I step out from the backrooms, adjusting my jeans, the thumping bass of the club fills the air, mingling with the scent of cheap perfume and sweat. I make my way toward the tables to watch the dancers, my eyes lazily scanning the stage, until they lock onto someone I never expected to see.

Nicole Everdeen.

The name sends a rush of dark memories through me, the sting of sorriness still fresh despite the months that have passed. She's the one who ripped my heart out, left me in pieces, and walked away without looking back. Here she is now, strutting her ass on stage like she owns the place, her body barely covered, showing off her curves to a room full of hungry eyes. The crowd watches her, their leers drinking her in like she's just another piece of meat.

My blood runs cold, but a twisted smirk pulls at my lips. So, little Miss Perfect is rebelling against daddy now? Didn't take long. Her old man had her under lock and key, always making sure his precious daughter never stepped foot into a place like this. Looks like she's finally showing her true colors. Just like I knew she would.

I pull out my phone, angling the camera perfectly to capture her up there, hips swaying, tits practically spilling out of her bra. She's putting on a show, and I make sure to get every angle of it. She wanted to run from me, act like I was the bad guy? Fine. It's my turn to remind her that nobody escapes me unscathed.

The photos are perfect. Clear and incriminating. She's going to hate me for this. That's the point though, isn't it?

With a few taps, I pull up her father's contact. Brickton Everdeen. I attach the photo, my fingers hovering over the send button for just a second, savoring the moment. She used to say I was an asshole, used to cry about how cruel I could be. Well, guess what, sweetheart? I'm living up to that now.

With a wicked grin, I hit send.

I don't give a damn what happens next. If she's lucky, her old man will drag her out of here before she completely embarrasses the family name. She played me once, but now I'm playing her, and I always win.

I tuck my phone back into my pocket, leaning back in my chair, watching her oblivious to what's coming. It's funny, really. She thought she could leave me behind, move on, but some scars never heal.

Chapter 2

Nicole

In the dressing room, I scrub off the last traces of stage makeup, watching as my reflection comes back into focus, a satisfied grin spreading across my face. The energy from the stage still hums in my veins. There's a thrill in dancing up there under the heat of the lights, moving in sync with the music while strangers' eyes track my every step. I can feel their hunger, the want etched into their faces, but there's a power in knowing they can't have what they crave. It's a freedom I was always denied, and each night I take the stage, it feels even better.

Dad always kept me on a tight leash, shaping me into his perfect vision of a good girl, always laying down rules, making sure I stayed in line. If only he knew. I'm not the obedient daughter he thinks I am. I'm up here claiming a piece of my life he can't touch, a part of me he'll never own. It's exhilarating, knowing I'm out here, night after night, and he has no idea.

He'd lose it if he knew. Right now, he thinks I'm hitting the gym, sweating it out at spin classes or yoga, playing the part of the dutiful daughter. Little does he know I'm sweating in front of an audience, on stage, earning my own money, every tip tucked away in my purse like a little act of defiance. It's not just the dancing; it's the irony that twists like a knife. For all his morals and rules, Dad's no saint. A few months ago, I stumbled on the truth about his so-called business. It's not just deals and handshakes, there's a darkness, the kind of dirty, bloody work that people pretend doesn't exist, and Maddox, my hard ass ex, was involved too. He was part of Dad's world all along. A brutal enforcer who walked through shadows I was never meant to see.

Dad might tell himself it's all justified, that he's cleaning up the streets, but the hypocrisy of it eats at me. He has blood on his hands while I'm not even allowed to make money on my terms. To hell with that. Now I strut my stuff at Dancing Babes, where the only judgment I get is on how I move and nothing more. For once, men look at me as something they desire, not a protected princess they can't touch. Here, my phone stays off; I'm untraceable, invisible to my father, my secret world safe for as long as I want it to be. I return home late, sweaty from the stage, so he's none the wiser on the nights he stops by my place. He'll never know what I'm up to unless I decide he should.

When I'm done scrubbing off my makeup, I slip into a pair of worn in Hey Dude's, stashing the night's tips deep in my purse. There's a drink calling for me at the bar before I head home, the lingering thrill of rebellion tingling in my veins. The night feels alive, each second stretching out as I savor the taste of freedom.

As soon as I reach the bar, a hand clamps down on my arm. My pulse skips, dread pooling in my stomach as I turn to face whoever's found me.

"Your dad is fucking pissed, Nicole," growls a voice from behind me, one that's all too familiar. My stomach twists as I turn and see Shephard, my father's vice president of his motorcycle club Black Shadows. Just the sight of him makes my pulse quicken in dread. This isn't just bad. This is about as horrible as it gets.

"How did he know I was here?" I try to keep my voice measured, even though my mind's racing. I was so careful, so sure I was untouchable.

"A little birdie sent him a photo of you with your tits out." He glares at me, shaking his head like I'm some rebellious kid who got caught sneaking out past curfew. "Now get your ass outside. You're coming with me."

I follow him out of the club, feeling all the thrill of my secret life crumble to dust. There's no way out of this, no easy excuse that'll save me now. Shephard leads me to his bike, the metal gleaming under the streetlights. With no other choice, I swing my leg over the back and wrap my arms around his waist as he guns the engine. The roar of it drowns out everything. The sound of the city and the thump of my heart. We speed off into the night, the cool wind biting against my cheeks, and I know the ride is only the beginning of what's coming.

As the city blurs past, my mind scrambles for any way I could have slipped up. I'd chosen Dancing Babes because it was out of town, where Dad's men wouldn't usually go. Clearly, I wasn't as hidden as I thought. Someone saw me, someone close enough to personally report back to him. Now, I have to face the consequences.

When we finally stop outside the warehouse, I don't wait for the engine to shut off before sliding off the bike, my heart pounding as I make my way up to the top floor. The office feels massive and imposing, the silence pressing down on me as I reach the door. Taking a deep breath, I push it open.

There he is, Brickton Everdeen, standing tall behind his desk. His face is shadowed, the lines of worry and anger stark under the dim light. His eyes lock onto mine, a storm of emotions swirling there. It's the scowl that confirms it. Shephard wasn't lying. Dad is furious.

"Nicole. What the fuck are you thinking?" he snaps, striding toward me with a fire in his gaze. Instead of the scolding I expected, he pulls me into a tight, crushing hug, holding on like he's afraid I'll slip away. The worry in his embrace nearly breaks me, and for a split second, I feel like a little girl again, safe in my father's arms. I can't stay there, can't let him think I'm still that girl. Gently, I push away, meeting his gaze with defiance.

"I'm making my own money, Dad. You won't let me do anything else," I say, standing my ground. "It's honest work."

"Honest work?" He steps back, frustration flickering in his expression as he runs a hand through his thick brown hair. "Letting men see you practically naked? Do you have any idea how disturbed I was to get those photos? Your pictures. On my phone."

The shame stings, a heat that creeps up my neck, but I force myself to hold steady. "To be fair, you weren't supposed to see it. That's why

I picked a club out of town, somewhere your guys wouldn't go."

"God damn it, Nicole," he sighs, and I can hear the anger draining, leaving only weariness and concern in his voice. "Why stripping, exotic dancing? Of all things, why that?"

I shrug, swallowing the lump in my throat as I search for the right words. "I like it. I'm good at it, and it's just dancing. Nothing more. No private rooms, no shady business. Just me, on stage. That's it. I swear."

He studies me, his gaze softening slightly, searching my face as if he's trying to find the girl he used to know. With a weary nod, he finally relents. "I believe you but damn, Nicole, you could have told me. Warned me. It was a shock to see that."

"And what would you have done?" I raise an eyebrow, challenging him. "You'd never have let me go through with it."

His jaw tightens, but he doesn't deny it. "No, I wouldn't have. I know you've been under lockdown since your mother died. Can you *blame* me?"

There's a crack in his voice, and suddenly, the tough, unbreakable man in front of me looks more vulnerable than I've ever seen. The tension drains from my shoulders, a sigh escaping before I can stop it. "I know, Dad. I get it. You're scared because you don't know who's out there. You think I'll be next."

He turns away, his voice breaking, barely more than a whisper. "I can't risk losing you too."

The rawness in his words catches me off guard, making me see him not just as the overprotective father who cages me in but as someone who's lost more than he ever should have. For a moment, all my anger slips away.

The worry in his voice hits me like a punch. I know how much he loves me, how terrified he is. I just want a taste of freedom. "Who sent you the photos?" I ask, trying to shift the conversation, needing to know who ratted me out.

He stares at me for a moment before speaking. "Nicole, don't do anything reckless."

"Dad, who sent it?"

His eyes flicker, and he looks away, as if saying it out loud would cause more pain. "Maddox."

The name sends a bolt of fury through me. My stomach twists, my hands balling into fists at my sides. "Maddox? That motherfucker."

"Nicole," Dad says, trying to calm me down, "he was just looking out for you."

"Looking out for me?" I laugh bitterly. "Or was he trying to get revenge because I broke up with him? Tell me, Dad, did he say he was doing it for my own good, or was it just payback?"

Dad winces, and I know I'm right. Maddox. Of course it was him. The petty bastard. He couldn't handle losing control over me, so he went and ruined everything.

"I hate him," I whisper, my voice shaking with anger. "I hate him so much."

Without another word, I storm out of the office, each step pounding like a drumbeat in my ears. My skin feels hot, flushed with anger, and I can still feel my father's words echoing in my mind. When I reach the parking lot, Shephard is leaning against his bike, arms crossed, watching me with a guarded look. He doesn't ask, doesn't pry, just waits.

"Take me to get my car," I snap, barely looking at him.

Without a word, he swings his leg over the bike and waits for me to climb on. The moment I wrap my arms around his waist, he guns the engine, and we roar out of the lot. The cool night air slaps against my face, sharp and biting, easing the edge of my anger but doing nothing for the knot still twisting in my stomach. I close my eyes against the rush of wind, trying to center myself, but the frustration simmers beneath the surface.

"He's just looking out for you," Shephard shouts over the engine, his voice rough but somehow kind.

"I know," I say back, though the words come out strained, my voice breaking. "But I still want to live my own life, Shep. Not in fear. You, of all people, can understand that."

I feel him nod, a small movement I only notice because I'm holding on to him. "Yeah," he replies, a softness in his tone. "That I can."

We pull into the night club's parking lot next to my car, but the sight that greets me sends my heart pounding all over again. Maddox's black Harley, complete with that obnoxious blue wolf insignia twisting around the tank, is parked right out front. My pulse quickens, anger prickling through me in fresh waves. He must be here, still inside gloating about what he's done, maybe thinking he's taught me some kind of lesson. The thought of that smug expression on his face makes my fists clench.

I don't hesitate. I glance over at Shephard, who watches me with a flicker of curiosity in his gaze but doesn't interfere. My fingers curl around the keys in my bag, the metal cool and solid in my hand. I stand over Maddox's bike, eyeing the wolf insignia. He's always loved this design, boasting about how it symbolizes strength and protection. But there's no honor in him. No loyalty. Just another weak man hiding behind a tough image.

Keeping my head low, I press the key against the gas tank, feeling the bite of metal on metal. With a steady, deliberate motion, I carve out the letters. Each drag of the key feels like a release, my anger channeled into the jagged lines forming under my hand. I dig deeper, harder, as I etch the last letter, watching as the paint scrapes away to reveal the rough metal beneath.

The word gleams raw against the sleek black tank, cutting right through that stupid wolf design. I take a step back, admiring the harsh edges, the way the letters slice through the image like a scar. He'll see it and know exactly who did it. Part of me wants to see his reaction, to watch the smugness fade from his face when he realizes just how far I'm willing to go. A bigger part of me knows what he's capable of, knows that I don't want to be around when he finds it.

I stand up, dusting my hands off and tossing my hair over my shoulder. As I head back to Shephard, his eyes flick from the scratched-up bike to me, a hint of amusement flickering in his gaze. He smirks, trying to hide the grin tugging at his lips.

He doesn't say a word, just gives me a nod as I walk past him and climb into my car, a small black Kia I love.

As I slide into the driver's seat, I catch Shephard's gaze lingering a moment longer than usual. There's an intensity in his eyes that makes my pulse skip, even though I know it's just a flicker, just a fantasy. Shep is undeniably handsome, rugged with his dark stubble, intense eyes, and broad shoulders. He's also my dad's VP, his most trusted man, loyal to the bone. Even if I entertained the thought, he'd never cross that line. Not for me. I push the idea away, brushing it off with a faint smile before putting the car into gear and backing out of the lot.

The drive home is quiet, a world away from the chaos I've left behind, but the tension in me doesn't fade. My grip on the steering wheel is tight, knuckles white as the adrenaline slowly starts to ebb. I replay the scene over in my mind. Shephard's unexpected arrival, my father's voice full of frustration, and that last bold act of rebellion against Maddox's bike. There's a thrill in it, a quiet satisfaction, but it doesn't entirely ease the knot of nerves in my stomach. I know Maddox. He's going to be furious. Furious and humiliated. A part of me, maybe a little twisted part, can't wait for him to feel it. I want him to taste that betrayal, to know what it's like to be on the receiving end of someone's scorn.

The glow of streetlights flickers past my window as I turn onto my street. The house looms up ahead, quiet and dark, casting long shadows across the lawn. I pull into the driveway, kill the engine, and sit for a moment, letting the silence settle around me. My phone sits beside me on the passenger seat, face-down. I know it's only a matter of time before Maddox calls or he storms over to confront me. Hell, he could already be on his way.

I don't touch the phone. I lean back, closing my eyes, breathing in the heavy quiet of the night. Outside, the crickets hum, a soft, monotonous drone that fills the void. It's calming, but not enough. The anger inside me is still there, simmering and waiting. It's like a coiled spring, taut and ready, needing just one more spark to set everything ablaze.

When I open my eyes, I stare up at the sky, a vast, endless black dotted with a few faint stars. The coolness of the night air presses in around me, and for a moment, I feel an eerie calm. It's strange, almost surreal, like standing on the edge of a cliff, looking down, waiting to see if you'll fall, or if someone will push you.

Chapter 3

Maddox

The night feels heavy as the bar empties, leaving me alone in the parking lot. A faint breeze drifts in, carrying the scent of stale beer and burnt rubber. Most of my guys have long since gone, peeling off to their wives or empty apartments, wherever they need to be. Me? I prefer to drown in my own damn misery out here.

I toss a leg over my bike, and just as I lean forward to fire up the engine, something catches my eye. A glint of silver etched across the gas tank. I frown, shifting closer to the tank so my drunk ass can see it better, and my stomach twists as I take in the word, scratched deep into the paint, slicing through the wolf I've had on my bike for years. *SNITCH.*

For a second, my brain doesn't register the letters, doesn't want to. Then it hits me like a punch to the gut, and a wave of fury rips through me, as hot and raw as an open flame. I know exactly who did this. Nicole. That fucking bitch. Of course it was her. No one else would dare pull something like this, not against me.

My hands tighten on the handlebars, knuckles whitening as the rage sharpens. I don't think. I don't check myself. I whip the bike around, tires screeching as I tear down the road toward her place, a single thought looping in my mind. She's going to pay for this. I don't notice the streetlights flashing by or the turns I'm making; it's like I'm running on instinct, a bullet shot from a gun, with only one target in my sight.

When I pull into her driveway, I spot the soft glow from her kitchen window, the light casting warm shadows through the curtains. Good. She's still awake. She better be.

I storm up to the door, my pulse pounding in my ears as I reach for the handle. Locked. Of course. I slam my fist against it, the wood rattling under the force of the blow. "Nicole!" I bellow, my voice echoing into the quiet of the night. "Open the damn door!"

Silence. Nothing. My blood is boiling, fists clenched, and without thinking, I rear back and punch the door. Pain shoots up my arm, but I don't care. The only thing on my mind is her, standing on the other side, probably laughing to herself. I go to hit it again, ready to break the damn thing down if I have to, but before I can, the door swings open.

There she stands, backlit by the light from the kitchen, her expression one of pure satisfaction. She's smirking, that same little smirk she's been flashing at me for years, taunting me like she's already won some game I didn't even know we were playing. Something snaps inside me. My vision blurs, and before I know it, I'm grabbing her by the throat, pushing her hard against the wall just inside her house, the door slamming shut behind us with a thunderous crash.

"Really?" I growl, voice tight with fury, watching her smirk falter as a flicker of fear crosses her eyes.

She sputters, her hands clawing at my grip. Her wide eyes meet mine, and for a brief second, I catch a glimpse of the girl I once loved, the one who tore me apart. I loosen my grip, releasing her, and she stumbles to the side, coughing as she rubs her throat. The fire in me hasn't dulled.

"You touched my bike," I snarl, voice low and controlled.

She straightens, coughing slightly, her expression shifting to something colder. "And you snitched on me to my dad," she spits out, her voice still hoarse but defiant. "Consider it even."

"Even?" I laugh, a dark, bitter sound that echoes in the empty room. "I didn't mess with your personal shit, Nicole. That bike's mine. You had no right to touch it."

I'm fucking drunk, the alcohol slurring the edges of my words, but my anger cuts through, sharp and searing. She broke me months ago, left me hollow and shattered, and now she's acting like none of it matters, like I was just some phase she's over.

Her eyes flash with defiance, that same fire that burned me alive once before. "Maybe next time you'll stay out of my business. You practically begged for it."

"You still don't get it, do you?" My voice cracks, and that slip, that weakness, only fuels my rage. "After all this, you don't get it."

She blinks, looking almost confused. "Get what, Maddox? That you're a controlling piece of shit who's mad because I moved on?"

The words cut deep, too deep. I grab her arm, maybe to steady myself, maybe to hold on to something real in the middle of the storm raging inside me. "You broke me, Nicole," I say, the words spilling out before I can stop them. "You didn't have to leave me like that. Like I meant nothing. Like I was nothing."

The admission feels like ripping open an old wound, one that never really healed. My finger jabs at my chest, the anger turning into something raw and vulnerable. "You were everything to me. Everything. You just walked away. So yeah, I took my shot when I could because I wanted you to feel it too. The emptiness. The hurt. Like I'm walking around dead inside."

The room falls into silence, my words hanging heavy between us. I've said too much, too honestly, and I don't know if I'd even want to take it back if I could. Her face softens, the defiance fading into something else. She reaches out, her hand sliding down to my wrist, her touch almost gentle as she pulls me toward the couch.

"Sit," she says, her voice softer now, the edge gone. I let her guide me, barely aware of myself as I collapse onto the couch, my limbs heavy, my vision blurring with exhaustion. It's like the fury is draining out of me, leaving only emptiness behind.

A moment later, she presses a glass of water into my hand. "Drink," she orders, her tone gentle but firm.

I push it away, the glass tipping over and spilling water across my lap. "Great. Look what you did," I mutter, slurring the words as I slump deeper into the couch, too tired to fight anymore.

"Shut up and drink, Maddox," she says, her voice a touch exasperated but patient as she brings the glass back to my lips. I drink, the water cool against my dry throat, grounding me even as the world spins.

The edges of my vision darken, the room fading into a comforting blur. Just before I lose myself completely to the blackness, I catch one last glimpse of her, her face soft, unreadable. I'm gone, swallowed up by the quiet that wraps around me like a cocoon, her voice fading into the background, a distant echo as I sink into darkness.

Fragments of last night flicker through my mind in pieces, like a broken film reel. I remember flashes of her silhouette leaning over me, her fingers working the blanket over my shoulders, tugging off my shoes and socks as she used to when things were good. There's a memory, or maybe just a fever dream of her sitting beside me, her face blurred as she nudged painkillers to my lips, her hands cool against my burning forehead as she forced water down my throat between slurred protests.

Everything spins, but one thing is crystal clear. I came here last night to make her feel the ache she left me with. instead, I stood there like a wreck, pouring out all my pain, the broken pieces of my heart laid bare for her to see.

The morning light is a knife slicing through the room, and I blink, disoriented, my head throbbing. I sit up, the blanket slipping from my shoulders and pooling in my lap. My throat's dry, raw, and the faint echo of last night's whiskey clings to my senses. As I rub my hands over my face, I notice her, slumped in the recliner across the room, hair tousled, her features softened by sleep. She looks like she used to when we'd curl up in that chair together, watching old movies until one of us finally nodded off, my arm draped over her shoulders.

The memories land hard, like a gut punch, and I tear my gaze away, a bitter knot tightening in my chest. Regret mingles with shame. I shouldn't have come here. Not drunk and hell bent on dragging her into my mess. I toss the blanket aside, silently sliding my socks and shoes on, my only goal is to slip out without waking her.

When I reach into my pocket, I feel nothing but the worn fabric and my phone. No keys. My stomach tightens. I scan the room, panic prickling beneath my skin as I search the couch, the side table, even glance around the front door thinking I dropped them. Still nothing.

I move into the kitchen, scanning countertops, pulling open drawers, fingers fumbling as the need to leave sharpens with every second. I come up empty. Damn it.

Just as I turn back toward the living room, my heart racing, I notice the recliner's empty. A soft hiss echoes down the hall from the bathroom. A second later, Nicole steps out, her expression hazy with exhaustion. Her gaze sweeps over me with that look she's perfected over the years. One that is half annoyed, half resigned. She lets out a small sigh, her shoulders dropping as she walks to the recliner, bends down, and reaches beneath it.

When she straightens, she's holding my keys, dangling them like a scolding parent dealing with a defiant child.

Our eyes meet, the silence thickening around us, heavy with all the things left unsaid. Her gaze is firm, but there's a sharpness there, something edged with anger, bitterness, and that lingering thread of hurt that neither of us can seem to shake. I take the keys from her, fingers brushing hers briefly, and swallow the rough knot in my throat.

"Thanks," I mumble, my voice rough, lower than I mean it to be. "And... sorry about last night."

Her expression barely shifts. If anything, her jaw sets tighter, a flash of resentment crossing her face, a reminder that my apology might mean nothing against the weight of everything that's come before. She's silent, doesn't even nod, just stands there, arms crossed, that bitter edge in her eyes cutting deeper than any words she could throw at me.

I turn away, the shame burning hot as I walk slowly, stepping outside and feeling the icy morning air slice through the last fog of alcohol. I climb onto my bike, turning to catch one last look at the house, my hand gripping the handlebar hard enough to make my knuckles ache. When I look up, she's still there, watching me with an unreadable expression, her arms crossed tightly over her chest like a shield.

"What?" I ask, the tension twisting into impatience, cutting through the lingering haze.

She narrows her eyes, her voice cold and hard. "Go fuck yourself, Maddox."

The words hang heavy, and before I can react, she turns on her heel, slamming the door shut behind her. The sound of the door slamming reverberates through me, a sharp echo of everything I've done wrong. The weight of my mistakes bears down like a storm cloud, suffocating and inescapable. I hang my head, dragging a hand through my hair, fingers tangling in frustration as I let out a long, shuddering breath.

I should leave. Every rational thought tells me to stay on my bike and disappear, but there's this pull, raw and relentless. A stupid, masochistic need to face her, to try again.

I swing off my bike and march back to her door. My heart thuds heavy and uneven as I twist the knob. It's unlocked. The tiny act of carelessness feels like an invitation, though I know better than to believe it.

The scent of brewing coffee greets me as I step inside. Nicole is in the kitchen, moving with a calm efficiency that feels like a slap in the face. She acts as if it's just another morning, as though I didn't storm in here drunk and unravel in front of her hours ago. Her back is to me, but the tension in her shoulders is unmistakable.

"I said I'm sorry," I say, my voice quiet but insistent. I move closer, the space between us charged and heavy. Her body stiffens, though she doesn't turn to face me.

"I heard you," she says, her tone clipped and controlled, the way it gets when she's barely holding onto her patience. She keeps her focus on the coffee machine as it drips, the silence between us thick enough to choke on. "But you can't undo what you've done. My dad is going to keep an even tighter leash now. So, thanks for that."

Her words cut deep, sharper than I'd expected. She pours two mugs with precision, her movements quick and almost mechanical, and shoves one into my hand. I take it, though my eyes stay on her, searching for any trace of the love she used to wear so openly. Her face is a fortress, every wall firmly in place.

"I fucked up," I admit, my voice dropping lower. "From the day your mom passed, I fucked up. Your dad and I, we were just trying to protect you. We tore the city apart looking for the bastard who killed her. We didn't want him coming for you next."

She shakes her head like she's trying to shake off the weight of my words. "I can't live my life in fear, Maddox. Not anymore. I spent two years with you and my dad smothering me, your men shadowing me every time I stepped out of the house. I just want to *live*." Her voice cracks on the last word, just barely, but it's enough to twist the knife already lodged in my chest.

"I get it," I say softly. "I do. But I couldn't stand by and do nothing. I couldn't lose you like—" My throat tightens, choking off the rest of the sentence. "I'm sorry if it felt like I was controlling you. I just... I wanted you safe."

I set the mug down on the counter, the clink of ceramic against granite too loud in the quiet kitchen. I take a step closer, closing the space between us. The smell of coffee hangs between us, bittersweet, a cruel reminder of simpler mornings long gone.

"I miss you," I say, the words barely audible, like confessing them might shatter what little thread is left holding us together.

For a moment, her gaze flickers to mine, and something soft, raw and unguarded flashes in her eyes. It's like catching a glimpse of sunlight through storm clouds. Then she blinks and it's gone, replaced by the cool detachment she's perfected.

"Finish your coffee and go, Maddox," she says, her tone steady and final. She places her own mug on the counter with a hollow thud, then turns and walks out of the room. The soft click of her bedroom door shutting behind her is louder than any scream.

I stare after her, feeling like the wind's been knocked out of me. No yelling, no fiery confrontation, just calm dismissal. It hurts worse than any anger she could have thrown my way.

I pick up the mug and drink, the bitterness burning down my throat as my mind replays her words, her expression, the crack in her voice. By the time I finish, the house feels emptier than when I arrived, and the weight in my chest tells me what I don't want to admit. I've lost more than just an argument. I might've lost her for good.

I storm out of Nicole's house, what was once my house, without looking back. The ride home blurs, the wind whipping past me, but it does nothing to clear the storm inside. My chest heaves, my heart hammering with every agonizing beat, a metronome of failure and regret. Each mile only fuels the inferno burning through me.

When I shove open my front door, the silence inside mocks me. It's too still, too suffocating. Something inside snaps, sharp and violent, and rage explodes out of me like a dam breaking. A guttural scream tears from my throat, raw and feral, as I grab the nearest thing, an old picture frame, and throw it with all my strength. The glass shatters against the wall, shards raining down like broken promises.

I don't stop. I can't. My hands grab anything in reach. Books, knickknacks, the vase Nicole picked out that I never liked. One by one, they meet the walls, the floor, the furniture. Each crash and crack fills the hollow ache inside me, if only for a second. My breath comes in short, harsh gasps, but it doesn't matter.

The TV is next. I grab the edge of it, lifting it with a strength born of fury, and slam it to the ground. The screen splinters, sparks flaring and dying like the last remnants of control I've lost. Glass crunches beneath my boots as I move to the kitchen, grabbing plates from the cabinet and sending them flying. The sound of ceramic smashing against tile is deafening, but it's not loud enough to drown out the voice in my head telling me what a colossal fuck up I am.

By the time I stop, the house is unrecognizable. The walls are dented, the floors littered with shattered pieces of what used to be my life. I'm breathing hard, chest heaving, my fists raw and trembling. The rage subsides, leaving only the heavy weight of regret and self-loathing in its wake. My knees threaten to buckle, but I force myself to stay standing.

The sharp buzz of my phone cuts through the haze. I dig it out of my pocket, glancing at the screen. *Jorge.* I hit the speaker and set it down on the counter, gripping the edge so hard my knuckles turn white.

"Hey," Jorge says, his voice too casual, too normal for the chaos surrounding me.

"What?" My voice comes out razor-sharp.

"Whoa, you good, boss?"

"Peachy," I spit, the word dripping with sarcasm, my throat raw from yelling.

There's a pause, the silence stretching just long enough to tell me Jorge knows something is off. "I was just checking in, but, uh... sounds like I got my answer. Want me to stop by?"

I glance around at the destruction, at the debris of my meltdown. The thought of anyone else seeing this makes my skin crawl. "Nah," I say, shaking my head even though he can't see me. "I'll be fine. See you tomorrow."

I hang up without waiting for a reply and toss the phone onto the counter, the clatter startling in the quiet. My hands are still trembling, the adrenaline slowly draining from my system. I look around the room, the wreckage surrounding me, and the weight of what I've done starts to settle in.

The broken glass catches the morning light, fragments glinting like tiny mirrors reflecting the mess I've become. I crouch down, picking up a piece of shattered ceramic, the edge cutting into my palm. The pain feels distant, almost welcome, a jarring counterpoint to the dull ache in my chest.

As I begin sweeping up the debris, I can't shake the realization that the damage goes deeper than the walls or the floors. The weight of everything I've broken feels heavier than anything I can clean up, and the worst part? I'm not sure I know how to fix any of it.

Chapter 4

Maddox

The crisp morning air bites at my face as I swing my leg over my bike and ride to the shop. The streets are still waking up; the world washed in pale gray as the sun struggles to break through the clouds. I wish the cold could do something about the storm raging in my chest, but no amount of icy wind can snuff out the fire I've been carrying since Saturday night.

Pulling into the lot, I kill the engine and step into the garage. The scent of motor oil and grease greets me, mingled with the faint metallic tang of machinery. It's grounding, this place. The clatter of tools and the hum of engines have always been my escape, the rhythm of work drowning out the chaos in my head. I grab a rag, wipe my hands instinctively, and dive under the hood of the first car waiting for me.

For a while, it works. Bolts, filters, and gaskets, it's all methodical. The satisfying click of tools against metal helps steady my hands and quiet my thoughts. I almost feel normal until the sound of boots scuffing against concrete snaps me out of it.

One by one, the crew filters in, their voices breaking the silence. I keep my head down, hoping to stay invisible, but Jorge is the last person on earth to take a hint. He saunters over; his trademark cocky grin plastered across his face.

"So," he starts, leaning against the side of the car like it's his personal bar stool, "want to tell me what the hell went down Saturday night?"

I twist the wrench on the air filter bolts, jaw clenched. "Not really."

Jorge lets out a low whistle. "You were pretty riled up when I called yesterday morning. Still pissy, huh? What happened at the club? You were there late. I left after midnight."

I exhale through my nose, irritated but trying to hold it together. "Saw Nicole."

"Oh." The word is drawn out, weighted with understanding. "Did her dad know?"

"Not at first."

Jorge sucks his teeth. "So... what'd you do?"

The wrench slips, and I grip it tighter, channeling my frustration into the tool. "Nothing worth repeating."

"That bad, huh?"

The muscles in my neck tighten. "Dude, *go work.*"

Jorge chuckles under his breath but thankfully moves off, giving me some space. I focus on the engine, but his words stick with me. My pulse pounds in my ears, and the heaviness in my chest only deepens.

After finishing up the job, I take the paperwork to Wylie at the front desk, forcing a smile as the customer thanks me and drives off. Another car pulls into the bay, Rich already popping the hood, but the thought of more work exhausts me. The rhythm of fixing things isn't fixing me today.

I retreat to the office, collapsing into the chair and kicking my boots up on the desk. The faint ticking of the wall clock grates on my nerves as I stare at the ceiling, waiting for some kind of answer, some way forward. Nothing comes.

I grab my phone and stare at Nicole's contact, the hesitation clawing at me. I need to say something, anything, but my gut twists at the thought of her rejecting me outright. Still, I hit call, holding my breath as the line rings.

Her voicemail picks up. That soft, familiar voice spills out: *"Hey, it's Nicole. You missed me, so leave a message, and I'll get back with you."*

The beep feels like a slap. Is she busy, or is she just done with me?

"Hey, Nic. It's Maddox." My voice sounds strained, awkward. I let out a nervous laugh, running a hand through my hair. "Uh, obviously, you know it's me. Look, I—" I stop, my throat tightening. "I just wanted to say I'm sorry. About everything. Can we talk? Please? I... I need to explain things. You know, while I'm sober." The words come out rushed, like if I don't say them fast enough, I'll lose my nerve. "Just call me back, okay? If you're willing. Um... bye."

I hang up, staring at the phone like it might combust in my hand. The silence that follows feels heavier than before. My head drops back against the chair, and I let out a long, frustrated sigh. All I can do now is wait.

After work, I head straight for the shower, stripping off my dirty clothes and boots as I go, leaving a messy trail through the house. The hot water beats down on my back, but it does little to temper the frustration simmering in my chest. I rub my hands over my face, hoping the steam might somehow clear my mind, but it's useless. When I step out and grab my phone, I notice the missed call from Nicole.

My heart lurches in my chest. My thumb hovers over her number for half a second before I hit 'call back'.

She picks up on the second ring, and the moment I hear her voice shaking, broken, and *crying*, I know something is wrong.

"Maddox..." she chokes out between sobs.

Adrenaline spikes through me, sharp and immediate. I'm already yanking on fresh clothes, my body moving on instinct. "What's wrong? What happened?"

"I need help," she whispers, her words trembling. "I'm at the club... hiding in the dressing room."

"Stay put. I'm on my way." I grab my keys and race out the door; the phone still clutched in my hand.

I'm on my bike in seconds, tearing out of the driveway like a bat out of hell. The roar of the engine drowns out the pounding of my heart as I weave through traffic, barely missing a car as I run a red light. Nothing else matters right now. The only thing in my head is Nicole, her voice, her tears, the fear laced in every word she said.

When I pull up to Dancing Babes, the neon lights flicker like a bad omen, casting eerie shadows against the dark street. I don't even notice the music thumping from inside or the bouncer's disapproving glare as I shove past him. My focus is singular.

I push through the crowd, ignoring the curious looks and drunken conversations around me. The smell of alcohol and sweat clings to the air, but I don't slow down. I pull my phone out again, dialing her number as I make my way to the back.

It rings once, twice, then she picks up. "Are you here?" she asks, her voice barely audible over the music.

"Yeah, baby. I'm right outside the dressing room," I say, my voice softening despite the tension coiled in my chest.

Seconds later, the door creaks open, and Nicole stumbles out. My heart nearly stops. Her makeup is smeared across her face, tear tracks cutting through the foundation, but it's the red, swollen mark spreading across her cheek and the corner of her eye that freezes me.

"Did someone fucking hit you?" I growl, my voice low and dangerous.

Her lip trembles as fresh tears spill down her face. She doesn't say a word, just collapses into me. My hands tremble as I cup her face, tilting it gently to get a better look at the damage. Rage boils beneath my skin, threatening to spill over, but I hold it back. She needs me calm right now, not out of control.

"Can we go?" she stammers, her body trembling against mine. Her voice is small and it shatters something deep inside me.

I grit my teeth, trying to keep my fury in check. "Who hit you, Nicole?"

Her breath hitches as she looks down, her hands clutching at my shirt like it's the only thing keeping her upright. "My boss... Art," she whispers, the name dripping with fear. "He wanted me to... entertain some men in the back. I told him no, and he... he slapped me. Hard. Then he shoved me into a room and forced me to..." Her voice breaks, and she doesn't finish. She doesn't have to.

The world around me seems to shatter. My fists clench, and a white-hot rage floods through me, threatening to explode.

I force it down for her.

I pull her into my arms, holding her tightly as she sobs into my chest. "I'm taking you out of here," I say, my voice hard.

With one arm around her, I lead her through the club, ignoring the stares and whispers as we push past the crowd. My mind races, already planning what I'm going to do to Art Remerick when I get my hands on him.

As soon as we're outside, I grab my phone and call her father. It rings twice before he picks up, the sound of machinery clanking in the background.

"I'm on my way. We have a fucking problem, Brickton," I snap before hanging up, not giving him a chance to respond.

Nicole clings to me as I mount the bike, her arms wrapping tightly around my waist. I can feel her shaking, her body pressed against mine, and it only makes my resolve stronger.

I rev the engine and tear out of the parking lot, weaving through the streets with her holding on like her life depends on it. My knuckles are white against the handlebars, my jaw clenched so tight it aches. The image of her bruised face flashes in my mind and the guilt twists in my gut.

I wasn't there when she needed me, but I'm here now, and Art is going to pay for every tear, every bruise and touch, every second of fear he put her through tonight.

My hand remains firmly around Nicole as we head upstairs to Brickton's office. Her body trembles against me, and I tighten my grip, silently promising her that no one will ever hurt her like this again. The door creaks as I push it open, stepping inside with her still by my side. Brickton is at his desk, reviewing papers, but the second his eyes land on Nicole and the bruise now marring her face, his expression darkens, turning a deep shade of red.

"What the hell happened?" he growls, storming over, fists clenched at his sides. His eyes flick between Nicole's tear-streaked face and mine, searching for answers, but there's only fury there.

I don't let go of her, keeping her close, feeling the weight of her pain in every trembling breath she takes. "Her fucking boss, Art," I say, my voice like gravel. "He hit her. Forced her into a room when she refused to entertain men. He...forced himself on her, Brickton." The words taste like poison on my tongue, and I can barely get them out without shaking. "I'm gathering my men. You may want to do the same because that bastard isn't walking away from this."

Brickton's eyes blaze with fury, a dangerous glint that matches the rage burning inside me. He doesn't hesitate, calling for his men with the kind of authority that shakes walls. The warehouse erupts into motion as they file in, each one ready for whatever comes next. It doesn't take long before my crew arrives too, the air thick with tension as we crowd into the office, plans forming quickly between gritted teeth and snarled words.

Brickton steps toward Nicole, his eyes softening for just a second as he looks at her. "You're safe now, sweetheart," he mutters, before turning back to me, his voice like steel. "We're hitting them hard."

I nod, the fire inside me still raging. "I'm not letting him get away with this. He touched her. Hurt her. He's going to fucking regret it." Even if Nicole and I aren't together right now, it doesn't matter. She's mine in every way that counts, and no one gets to put their hands on her and walk away.

The plan is simple yet brutal. Two of Brickton's men and one of mine will stay back, holding down the fort and keeping Nicole safe while the rest of us flood Dancing Babes like a storm to deal with the Steel Wings. There's no hesitation, no second thoughts. This is what we do. This is who we are. They crossed a line, and now they'll pay for it in blood.

As I stand there, surrounded by men ready for war, Nicole's presence at my side grounds me. My hand still rests on her waist, a silent promise. She may not be mine right now, but in my heart, she always will be. Anyone who dares to hurt her will feel the full weight of that claim.

Chapter 5

Maddox

There are over three dozen of us when we roll into the club parking lot, the low growl of engines signaling the crusade that's about to hit. The night air is thick with tension, the kind that crackles along your skin. The lot is nearly empty, just the way we need it. Fewer customers means less chance of innocent casualties when the gunfire erupts. It's coming. We all know it. I can feel the adrenaline buzzing through my veins, my fingers twitching toward my gun.

I move with Brickton at my side, both of us cutting through the dim lot like predators. We aren't just men, we're legends in the Phoenix MC world. The patches on our cuts announce our presence as much as the rumble of our bikes. People around here know who we are; they know better than to cross us. Tonight, though, Art made the mistake of touching Nicole, and now we're bringing the fury of two MC clubs down on him.

As we push through the front doors, the noise of the club hits us. Loud music thumping, glasses clinking, but it doesn't faze us. We cut through the thin crowd, past patrons who barely look up. A few bouncers see us and tense, stepping forward like they might have a shot at stopping us.

Big mistake.

Brickton and I both draw our guns, the cold metal of the grip fitting perfectly in my hand. I aim it squarely at the first bouncer who freezes, fear flickering in his eyes. "Where's Art?" I growl, my voice low and deadly.

The man's face goes pale as he points upstairs, too scared to do anything else. We move fast, storming up the steps like a hurricane about to crash down. My heartbeat pounds in my ears, the image of Nicole's tear-streaked face and the bruise on her cheek fueling every step I take.

When we kick the office door open, the scene inside turns my stomach. Art is behind his desk, a woman on her knees in front of him, her head bobbing as he grins like the sick bastard he is. The girl jumps up at the sight of us, scrambling to fix her top before running out of the room in a panic. Art tucks his pathetic excuse of a dick back into his pants, his cocky grin faltering when he sees the army of men filling his office.

"What the fuck is the meaning of this?" he barks, his voice trembling just a little.

Brickton steps forward, his anger rolling off him in waves. "You touched my daughter tonight," he growls, and I see the color drain from Art's face.

"I don't know what you're talking about," Art stammers, glancing around like he's looking for a way out. "I've been with several girls tonight. Maybe you've mistaken me for someone else."

My blood boils, and I step forward, aiming my gun at his forehead. "You forced yourself on Nicole. She works here, dances here. You wanted her to do more, didn't you? You wanted her to entertain your sleazy fucking clients, and when she refused, you punished her. You raped her."

My words are cold, each one cutting like a blade. I also know that in that same breath, I called myself a lowlife, using women for my own pleasure, but I never forced them like he did.

Art's eyes widen, panic setting in as he stammers, "No, no, that's not what happened. She was just learning how to keep customers interested. That's all. Many men have shown interest in her."

The gun feels heavy in my hand, the weight of it begging for action. I cock it, the sound loud in the room, and press it hard against his forehead. My finger tightens around the trigger. "You're a fucking liar."

His hands shoot up, palms out in a pathetic plea. "I'm sorry! I was just trying to help her make more money, that's all. She's a good girl, I swear. Please, don't—"

One glance at Brickton and his nod is all the confirmation I need. My finger squeezes the trigger, and the shot rings out like thunder. Art's brains splatter across the wall behind him, and his body slumps lifelessly to the floor.

I turn on my heel, leaving the chaos behind me without a second glance. The air around me feels charged, heavy with unspoken tension, as my men follow in silence. Each footfall echoes off the stairwell walls as we descend to the main floor, where the rest of the crew waits.

The once crowded bar is now eerily quiet. The patrons have been cleared out, ushered into the night like cattle fleeing a storm. All that remains are Art's men, corralled in the center of the room. They stand stiff, shoulders squared but eyes darting, their expressions shifting between confusion and fear. They know something's coming, they just don't know what.

I stride across the room, every step intentional, my boots heavy against the stained concrete floor. My gun, still warm from earlier, rests in my hand, the weight of it grounding me as I stop in front of the first man in line.

He's young, barely older than a teen, his face pale and slick with sweat. I lift the gun, pointing it squarely at his chest. He flinches, his breath hitching as he stares down the barrel.

"Why follow a man who rapes women?" My voice cuts through the silence like a blade, each word dripping with disgust.

The kid shakes his head frantically, his eyes wide and pleading. "I didn't know, I swear. I had no idea." His voice cracks, desperation spilling out in every syllable.

I narrow my eyes, searching his face for any sign of deceit. The truth is, I don't care if he knew or not. He's part of this, complicit in the rot Art spread through this place. Still, I give him a chance. A slim one.

"Make sure his extracurriculars stay gone," I snap, my tone sharp as a whip. "Or you'll be next."

"Yes, sir," he stammers, nodding so fast it's a wonder his neck doesn't snap. Relief floods his face when I lower the gun, but I don't miss the way his hands tremble.

Satisfied, I turn and motion for my men to follow. We're almost at the bikes when the sharp crack of a gunshot tears through the night.

The sound reverberates through my skull, and before I can react, Tip, the man who's been by my side for years, drops to the ground.

Time seems to freeze. For a moment, all I can hear is the dull roar of blood rushing in my ears. Then the rage hits, white-hot and all consuming.

I whip around, my gun raised as my men, as well Brickton's, do the same, unleashing hell back toward the club. The night erupts in chaos of shattering windows, the screech of gunfire ripping through the air, and shouts of panic mingling with the metallic tang of blood.

Every shot I fire is deliberate, fueled by the fury coursing through my veins. One by one, the Steel Wings members fall. The faces of Art's men blur together, their bodies dropping like dominoes. They had their chance to walk away. They chose to fight.

When the dust settles, silence envelops the night once more. The acrid stench of gunpowder lingers, mixing with the metallic scent of blood. My chest heaves as I take in the scene of broken glass glittering on the floor, bullet riddled walls, and the lifeless bodies of the Steel Wings men scattered like discarded trash.

It's over but it doesn't feel like a victory.

I turn around and the sight of Tip's body hits me like a sledgehammer to the gut. His lifeless eyes stare up at the night sky, his blood pooling beneath him. He was one of the best. Loyal, fierce, and a man I trusted with my life. Now he's gone.

The weight of what I have to do next crushes me, but I don't have a choice.

The headlights of my bike cut through the darkness as I pull up to Colt Tipton's house. The quiet street feels suffocating, the stillness mocking the storm raging inside me. I kill the engine and sit there for a moment, staring at the modest home where Tip built a life with a wife and two kids. He loved his family more than anything.

The porch light flickers on, and I know Layla's already waiting. Wives like her always know.

Jorge steps up beside me, silent and somber. I don't need to look at him to feel the weight of his presence. He's here to support me, but nothing can make this easier.

I knock on the door, the sound too loud in the still night. It doesn't take long before it creaks open.

Layla stands there, holding their infant son against her chest. Her face is pale, her eyes tired but dry. She doesn't cry, doesn't flinch, just looks at me with a quiet resolve that makes my chest ache.

"Is he dead?" she asks, her voice flat and numb.

I nod, my throat tightening. "Yeah, he is."

"How?" Her gaze doesn't waver, though I can see her grip on the baby tighten.

"Shot," I say, my voice heavy. "Taking down men who hurt women. He died doing the right thing."

She nods, biting her lip as she swallows hard. There's no wail of grief, no dramatic outburst. Just a quiet, "Damn it."

I want to say something more, to offer comfort or some kind of reassurance, but the words die in my throat. Nothing I say will bring him back.

"I'm sorry, Layla," I manage, my voice raw. "Whatever you need, you let me know. I'm here. Always."

Her lips press into a tight line as she gives me a small, almost robotic nod. "Thanks, Maddox."

Without another word, she closes the door.

The sound echoes in my ears as I turn back to Jorge, the weight of the night pressing down on me like a thousand bricks.

"She's tougher than all of us," Jorge murmurs, his voice low.

"Yeah," I say, my voice hollow. "But she shouldn't have to be."

Jorge glances at me as we walk back to our bikes, but he doesn't say anything else. He knows there's nothing to say. He heads home, and I make my way back to the warehouse where Nicole sits with Brickton, his vice president Shephard, and my man Geoffrey. The tension is thick when I walk in. Nicole looks fragile, her eyes red from crying, but as soon as she sees me, she stands up, her body moving toward me instinctively.

"Thank you for coming to me so quickly," she says softly, her voice full of a gratitude that stings more than it soothes.

I take her hand without thinking, leading her to the break room. The place is mercifully empty, just the hum of the fridge filling the silence. I turn to her, tilting her chin up so her tear-streaked face meets mine. She's still beautiful, even in her pain. Always has been.

"We may not be together anymore, but that doesn't mean I want anything bad to happen to you," I say, my voice rougher than I intend. "You can always call me. I'll always be here."

Her bottom lip trembles, and she nods, another tear slipping down her cheek. "I'm sorry for the way we ended. I didn't want it to be like this."

"Me too, Nicole." My chest tightens as I gently kiss her forehead, the lingering scent of her perfume taking me back to a time when things were simpler. When she was mine.

We stand there for a moment, the silence between us thick with things we'll never say. Then, I let her go.

I head out with Geoffrey, both of us silent as we ride back to our homes. The wind whips against my face, but it doesn't numb the ache in my chest. I'll sleep tonight, maybe, but tomorrow, the same routine will start again. Running the mechanic shop, pretending like everything's normal, like I'm not broken inside from losing her.

There's something I cling to though, a small sliver of hope. She called me. Of everyone in her life, she called *me* when she was in trouble. Maybe it means something. Maybe it's enough to get me through the days ahead, even if it doesn't erase the hurt.

Months blur by in a haze of work, violence, and numbness. My days are filled with fixing cars at the shop, taking out scumbags who prey on the innocent, and nights spent at a new club where I drink until I can't feel anything, fucking woman after woman just to forget. It's February now, and the holidays came and went in a blur. I spent Christmas with my mother, going through the motions of family life. Nicole hasn't spoken to me since that night I rescued her, and I've given up on thinking she ever will.

Brickton and I still work together, and every now and then, he updates me on how Nicole's doing. He put her in counseling, which has helped her start to reclaim her life, at least a piece of it. The tough, fearless biker chick I once knew is now a fragile shell, but she's getting stronger. Brickton says she's getting out of bed more often, that she doesn't flinch at every little noise or movement anymore. Still, it hurts to know what she's gone through, and the thought of her being broken like that eats away at me.

Meanwhile, Brickton and I, along with our men, took down two more MCs running child trafficking rings. We stormed in before those sick bastards could sell the kids off, saving them from a nightmare and returning them to their families. The news still calls us vigilantes, faceless heroes trying to right the wrongs of the world. There's power in that, knowing we've saved lives. Every time I pull the trigger, every time I end another scumbag, I lose a little more of myself.

It's like a piece of my soul is chipping away with every kill, every bottle of liquor, every faceless woman I fuck just to fill the void Nicole left behind. I wonder if there's any part of me left that she'd even recognize.

I am elbow deep in an alternator, hands greasy and mind numb, when a sedan pulls up. My heart stops for a second as Nicole steps out, smiling softly at my men as she walks toward the shop. She hasn't been here since we broke up over a year ago.

I straighten up, wiping my hands on a rag. "Give me a few and I'll be out," I call to her, trying to sound calm even though my pulse is racing.

"I'll be in your office," she says before disappearing inside, her voice carrying that same softness, like she's testing the waters.

I finish up the car in record time, trying to focus on the task at hand but failing miserably. After handing the paperwork to Wylie and thanking my customer, I make my way to the office. When I walk in, Nicole is standing there, staring at the pictures on my wall. The ones I never had the heart to take down. Photos of us, back when things were good, back when we were something.

"Hey," I say from the doorway, leaning against the frame, trying to play it cool.

She turns around quickly, almost like she's been caught doing something she shouldn't. "Hi Maddox," she says, her voice soft but firm. Her brown hair is longer. Her chestnut eyes focused on me.

There's a long silence as we just look at each other, the air thick with everything we haven't said. She looks good, better than she did the last time I saw her, but there's still a heaviness in her eyes. It reminds me that she's still healing, still working through the damage.

I wonder if I'm part of that damage.

"You look... good," I say, stepping further into the office, unsure of how to bridge the gap between us.

"Thanks," she replies, her gaze flicking back to the photos. "You still have these up."

I rub the back of my neck, feeling a little embarrassed. "Yeah. Didn't feel right taking them down."

She smiles softly, but it doesn't quite reach her eyes. "I wasn't sure if I'd ever come back here."

I swallow hard, unsure of what to say. Part of me wants to apologize again, to tell her how sorry I am for everything that happened. The other part of me knows that words don't mean shit anymore.

"I'm glad you did," I finally say.

"I wasn't sure if I could face you," she admits, her voice wavering slightly. "But I wanted to try. I wanted to thank you."

"For what?"

"For that night," she says quietly, meeting my eyes. "For saving me when I couldn't save myself."

There's a lump in my throat as I nod, my chest tightening. "I'll always come for you, Nicole. Always."

She looks at me for a long moment, like she's weighing something in her mind. Then, she steps closer, and for the first time in what feels like forever, she reaches out and touches my hand. "I know," she whispers.

It's a small gesture, but it feels like the beginning of something. Maybe not the way we used to be, but something new. Something that can heal, just like she's healing.

Chapter 6

Nicole

I can see it in Maddox's eyes, the flicker of hope, faint but undeniable. It's that same look he used to give me when we were younger, back when the world felt simpler, back when I thought he was my forever. His gaze clings to me now, filled with a quiet yearning that makes my chest tighten.

Even if we can't go back to what we were, Maddox is still the only person I trust with this. He's the only one who won't dismiss me, won't write me off as some grieving daughter clutching at straws.

"I need your help Maddox," I say, breaking the silence as I let go of his hand. The weight of the room seems to shift, pressing down on me. The air feels thick, like it's holding its breath, waiting for what comes next.

His eyes narrow slightly, not with suspicion but with concern. "With what?" His voice softens, his tone gentle in a way that makes me want to crumble.

When he steps closer and tilts my chin up, forcing my gaze to meet his, I feel that pull. It's strong, magnetic, and dangerous. It's the same connection that's always been between us, even when I tried to convince myself it was gone.

"I've been digging into my mom's case," I confess, my voice trembling. "Her murder. Some of the reports don't add up. Small details, inconsistencies that might mean nothing, but they might mean everything." The words spill out in a rush, and I feel exposed, like I've just handed him the most fragile part of myself.

His brow furrows, and the intensity of his stare pins me in place. "Have you told your dad?"

"Not yet," I admit, shaking my head. "I need to be sure first. He'll dive in headfirst, and I'm not ready for that yet. I just... I need to know if I'm seeing ghosts or if there's actually something there."

His jaw tightens as he processes my words, and then he nods, his resolve hardening in that way I remember all too well. "What can I do, Nicole?"

The way he says my name. It's low, steady, and grounding. I feel a flicker of relief, but also a pang of something deeper, something more dangerous. He's pulling me in without even trying.

"Look through it all with me," I say, my voice quieter now, almost unsure. "Tell me if I'm crazy or if I'm onto something real."

His answer is immediate. "Sure. I can do that. I'll come by after work."

Relief washes over me, but it's quickly followed by a rush of anxiety. "I'll order supper," I say, my tone clipped, trying to keep things casual, trying to keep my walls up. "See you soon, then."

I leave his office before I can change my mind, before I can let myself do something reckless, like lean into him, like kiss him. My heart pounds in my chest as I walk away, and I can feel his eyes on my back, heavy and unrelenting.

The pull between us is undeniable, a force that's always been there, no matter how hard I've tried to sever it. This isn't about us. This is about my mom.

Still, as I climb into my car and grip the steering wheel, I can't stop my mind from wandering. Can we really keep our past buried? Or will this crack in the surface be all it takes for everything to come rushing back?

Just before five, a knock echoes through my house. I glance at the clock and smirk. "You're early," I call out, expecting Maddox's familiar swagger on the other side. When I swing the door open, my smile freezes mid curve.

Standing on my porch is not Maddox. It's Shephard.

"What are you doing here?" My voice falters as unease coils in my chest. I instinctively take a step back, but Shephard presses forward, pushing his way inside like he owns the place. His presence is oppressive, heavy, and it drags the air out of the room with it.

"You're seeing Maddox again? Why?" His tone is cold, clipped, and the sharpness of his glare cuts through me.

I force myself to stay calm even though my pulse is racing. "We're not seeing each other. We're just talking as friends. What do you want, Shep?"

My deflection doesn't work. His eyes narrow, and something dark flickers behind them, something I don't recognize but instantly fear. "A little birdie told me you went to see Maddox today. Asking for his help about your mom's case."

The blood drains from my face. Maddox and I had been careful. We hadn't told anyone about our conversation, or so I thought.

"So, what if I did?" I scoff, trying to sound braver than I feel. "It's my mom. I have every right to dig into what happened to her."

He steps closer, looming over me, and the menace in his voice makes my stomach churn. "You need to stop digging, Nicole. Drop it. Walk away. This is your only warning."

"And if I don't?" I challenge, though my voice comes out quieter than I intended.

Shephard leans in, his breath hot against my face, his tone dropping to a deadly whisper. "Then you'll be burying Maddox next."

The weight of his words hits me like a sledgehammer. My legs threaten to buckle, but I stand my ground, refusing to give him the satisfaction of seeing me crumble.

He doesn't wait for a response. He turns and leaves, slamming the door behind him with enough force to rattle the walls.

The second he's gone, I collapse onto the floor, my knees giving out as the adrenaline drains from my body. My hands shake uncontrollably as I press them to my face, trying to make sense of what just happened.

It's all starting to make sense now. The unanswered questions, the loose threads I hadn't been able to tie together. My mom's murder wasn't random. Shephard's involved, the way he's trying to shut me down, it all points to something bigger and darker than I'd ever imagined.

Panic surges through me as I grab my phone and call Maddox. It goes straight to voicemail. "Maddox, it's me. Don't come to my house. Shephard's onto us. Call me when you get this."

I hang up, but the gnawing fear doesn't ease. I can't wait for him to call back. What if Shephard is out there waiting, watching for him? What if this is a trap?

Snatching my keys, I sprint to my car. My tires squeal as I back out of the driveway, taking the back roads, the quickest way to Maddox's route from his shop. My hands grip the steering wheel so tightly my knuckles ache.

Finally, I spot him, his bike a gleaming silhouette in the fading sunlight. Relief washes over me as I flash my headlights and lay on the horn, catching his attention.

He pulls a sharp U-turn and follows me into an alley, secluded and quiet. My heart slams against my ribs as I throw the car into park and jump out.

"Maddox," I run straight into his arms, my voice trembling with panic. "You have a traitor in your club. So does my dad. I think I've figured out my mom's murder, and now they're coming for us."

His arms tighten around me, a fleeting moment of safety, before he pulls back, his hazel eyes narrowing in confusion and alarm. "What the hell are you talking about?"

"Shephard showed up at my house," I rush out, my words tumbling over one another. "He knew I talked to you. He threatened to kill you if we're seen together. Someone in your crew tipped him off. Someone at your shop today."

"Fuck," Maddox growls under his breath, running a hand through his hair. His jaw clenches as he scans the alley, his body tense, like he's ready for a fight.

"Listen to me, Nic." His voice is commanding. "Go home. Lock your doors. Don't let anyone in until I call you. I'll handle this. I'll talk to your dad, and we'll figure out who's playing us."

"Maddox, please. You don't know who you can trust anymore." My voice cracks, the fear bubbling over.

His eyes soften, just for a moment, as he grips my shoulders. "Don't worry about me. Worry about staying safe. I'll take care of this."

I hug him tightly, clinging to him for a fleeting moment of comfort before forcing myself to pull away. As I drive home, my mind races, the puzzle pieces snapping together at an alarming speed.

My mother's death wasn't random. It was calculated. Now, because I'm getting too close, the people who killed her are coming after Maddox, and possibly me.

The moment I get home, I rush to the kitchen and fling open my bag, pulling out the stack of papers I've been carrying around like lifelines. I spread them across the table, the pages curling slightly at the edges as they scatter. Each one holds a fragment of the timeline I've been piecing together for two years. Police reports, coroner's notes, and my own scribbled observations. I run my fingers over them, connecting dots no one else seems to have noticed.

The weight of Shephard's threat lingers like a dark cloud over me, and for the first time, I see the full picture. It's terrifyingly clear now. The lies and betrayals all spiral back to that one horrific night when my mother was murdered. This isn't just about her anymore. It's about Maddox, my dad, and me.

I try to settle my paced breathing as I tell myself Maddox will be fine. He said he'd talk to my dad, and together they'll unravel this mess before anyone else gets hurt. Maddox is smart. Strong. He won't let them win.

Deep down, a hollow pit of dread twists in my stomach. This isn't over. I know it, and so do they. The danger is only beginning.

The evening stretches into a suffocating night, the hours crawling by as I sit at the table, unable to leave the scattered papers behind. Every creak of the house sets me on edge. Every shadow outside the window makes my skin prickle. I call Maddox once, then twice, then so many times I lose count. Each unanswered ring sends my mind into darker places.

By midnight, the silence has become unbearable, like a weight pressing down on my chest. I tell myself he's okay, that he's just caught up in sorting everything out. As the hours slip away and dawn breaks in pale streaks of light, my hope begins to fracture.

Something is wrong.

I grab my keys, my hands trembling, and drive to my dad's house. The streets are eerily quiet, a stillness that feels foreboding, like the calm before a storm. By the time I reach his front door, I'm pounding on it so hard my knuckles ache.

When he finally answers, he's in his robe, his face groggy but quickly sharpening with concern when he sees me. "Nicole? What's going on?"

"Dad, something bad has happened." My voice cracks, and the fear I've been choking down all night surges to the surface. "Maddox was supposed to call me after he talked to you last night. I haven't heard from him. I think... I think they got to him first."

His brow furrows, confusion and alarm flashing across his face. "Who? Nicole, slow down. Who are you talking about?"

"Shephard," I whisper, the name tasting like poison on my tongue. "And whoever else is playing both of you. Someone is a traitor in your club, Dad, and in Maddox's. Someone has been feeding them information, keeping tabs on everything."

His eyes widen, and the shift in his expression is instant. Confusion gives way to grim understanding. He steps aside and motions me in.

We sit at the kitchen table, the same spot where I used to do homework as a kid, but now the air is heavy with a bodement I've never felt before. I lay everything out for him. Shephard barging into my house, his threat to kill Maddox, the years I've spent piecing together my mom's murder, and how it all seems to lead back to the clubs.

My dad listens, his face darkening with every word. By the time I finish, his hands are clenched into fists on the table. "Nicole…" He exhales slowly, shaking his head as if trying to process it all. "Don't tell anyone else about this. Not yet. Let me dig into it. I'll find out what's really going on, and I'll find Maddox, but you need to stay out of it, understand?"

I nod, but the reassurance in his words feels thin, like rubber stretched too far.

As I drive home, the fear doesn't abate. If anything, it worsens. I keep calling Maddox, my thumb trembling as I hit redial repeatedly. Every time it rings out into nothingness, the hollow pit in my chest grows.

By the time I crawl into bed around noon, exhaustion has wrapped itself around me, but sleep is impossible. My mind won't let me rest, replaying Shephard's threat and Maddox's promise to handle it. What if he didn't get the chance? What if they killed him?

The thought spirals, gaining momentum until it becomes unbearable. My chest tightens, and tears spill over, hot and unrelenting. Worse still is the fear that he died thinking I don't care, that he doesn't know how much I still love him.

I bury my face in the pillow, sobs shaking my body as the weight of it all crashes over me. The past isn't just catching up to us, it's pulling us under, and I don't know if I can fight my way to the surface before it's too late.

Chapter 7

Maddox

Pain pulses through my skull as my vision sharpens, dragging me back into consciousness. A dim, flickering light sputters overhead, casting shaky shadows across the cement walls of the room I'm in. It's cold, damp and the unmistakable basement of Brickton's warehouse. *How the hell did I end up here?*

I blink hard, trying to gather my scrambled thoughts. I came here last night to talk to Brickton about spies in our clubs. He seemed anxious, his face tight with worry, like he was already expecting bad news. I was mid-sentence when someone opened the office door behind me. I turned to see who it was, and then… nothing. Everything went black until now.

I curse under my breath. *Please don't tell me Brickton was involved in his wife's murder.* It doesn't make sense. They were the ideal couple. They never fought, always looked so damn in love. Why would he have her killed?

My chest tightens. Nicole is waiting for me. I was supposed to call her after I spoke to her father. She doesn't even know what kind of danger we're in. She doesn't know that her father might be tangled in this mess deeper than I ever imagined.

Right now, I have to focus on getting out. The one advantage I have is that I know this place like the back of my hand. I know something Brickton's men clearly didn't think about. There are no cameras down here. No eyes on me. I can slip out unnoticed.

I force myself to my feet, wincing as the pain throbs in my head. The door to this room is old, barely hanging on its rusty hinges. I press my shoulder against it, testing the lock, and with the right angle and a solid shove, it pops open. *Amateur move, Brickton.*

My pulse quickens as I move quietly through the basement, navigating the narrow, damp corridors. There's no sound, no sign of movement. Good. The warehouse is empty during the day. Brickton's crew only operates under the cover of night. From the outside, it's just a business that makes metal signs. Beneath the surface, it's a front for something much darker. Our way of taking out predators who prey on children. And now, the place that's been a fortress for justice is holding me captive.

Not for long.

I make it to the door leading up to the ground floor, carefully working the handle until it gives way. The cold metal creaks softly, but not loud enough to draw attention. If anyone is even here. As I slip through, I stay low, weaving through the massive machinery that lines the warehouse floor. My senses are on high alert, every instinct screaming at me to move faster but stay sharp. If Brickton has men here, I can't risk being seen.

I reach the side door, adrenaline surging through me as I push it open just enough to slip outside. The cold air hits me like a slap to the face, but it's a welcome shock. I'm free.

My bike's parked just outside the warehouse, and by some miracle, they didn't check my pockets for my keys. I thank whatever God is on my side this morning, jump on, and gun the engine. The roar of the bike cuts through the silence, and I don't waste a second. I peel out of the lot and race toward Nicole's place.

She has no idea how close she is to being caught in this nightmare. I have no idea how much time I have left before they realize I'm gone.

As I pull up to Nicole's house, she runs out, flinging the door open before I even get off my bike. Her face is pale, her eyes wide with worry.

"Where the hell were you?" she demands, holding out a hand to stop me from coming closer as I walk up her porch.

"Your dad and one of his men knocked me out. He put me in the damn basement," I say, my voice tight with frustration. "I just woke up and got out. We need to leave now. It's not safe here."

Nicole's face goes slack with shock for a second before she regains her composure, nodding. She disappears inside, grabbing her purse as I down a glass of water in the kitchen. The clock is ticking, and we both know it.

We lock up and I start my bike, her arms wrapping around me tightly as we tear through the empty streets. I push the bike hard, flying past streetlights until we reach the edge of town. I know exactly where to go, my mother's place, a few towns over. No one will expect us to be there.

When we pull into the driveway, my mom steps out on the front porch, eyes wide in confusion. I shout over the engine, "Open the garage."

She rushes to press the button, and I pull in quickly, hiding the bike behind the closed door. As soon as we step inside the house, my mom comes up to Nicole, embracing her tightly. "It's good to see you, Nicole. It's been too long."

"You too," Nicole whispers, but her voice cracks, and suddenly she's crying.

She leans into me, her tears soaking through my shirt. My mom looks at me, clearly puzzled, and I give her a dour look as we move into the kitchen.

Once seated at the table, I spill everything. The ambush, Brickton's possible involvement in his wife's death, the threat Nicole received from Shephard. As I speak, Nicole grows quieter, her face pale but her mind clearly working. Then she asks the question I know has been eating at her.

"If my dad was involved... does that mean he had my mom killed?" Her voice is barely a whisper.

I exhale deeply, unable to lie to her. "It looks that way. I'm sorry, Nicole. I never saw this coming, and I had no idea."

She takes a shaky breath, her eyes flicking to the oversized purse she brought along. "I thought I had it all figured out before, but adding my dad into the mix changes everything." She pulls out a file, thick with notes and clippings, and spreads it on the table. "There's more. So much more."

I sit up straight, eyes narrowing. "What do you mean?"

Nicole opens the file, laying out a meticulously organized timeline of incidents surrounding her mom's death. "Shephard's threat to you finally connected all the dots. Someone broke into my parents' house a few months before my mom's murder. Then, there were two other incidents. Someone almost ran her down while she was shopping, and about a month before she was shot, she told me a motorcyclist was following her. She never got a good look at them, but she was sure they were trailing her. She'd said it was a woman because they had long hair, with nothing on that identified them to a club."

Nicole spreads out the papers, pointing to each event with trembling fingers. "Now I think it wasn't a woman on the bike. What if it was Geoffrey? He has a ponytail, Maddox. He's one of your most trusted guys. He was the first to ask why I was at your shop yesterday. What if he already knew?"

I stand abruptly, nearly knocking my chair over. "No. It couldn't have been Geoffrey. He's loyal. He'd never turn on me." I pace the room, trying to shake the image of my closest friend as a traitor. "He can't be involved."

Geoffrey has been my friend since high school, a constant presence through every twist and turn of my life. He was a loyal member of the club back when my father was president and has stood by me through thick and thin. I can't imagine him being involved in something like this, but as I sift through Nicole's timelines, police reports, and news clippings, the evidence paints a picture I can't ignore.

Nicole's eyes darken as she points to the day her mother died. "My dad was devastated, Maddox. He could barely breathe, or so I thought. What if he was faking it? What if his guilt was eating him alive? At her funeral, he couldn't even look at me. I thought he was just grieving but what if it was something else?"

I pause, staring at her. "But why? Why would he do this?"

Nicole takes a deep breath, her voice trembling. "My mom begged him to stop the vigilante work, though at the time, I didn't even realize that's what she meant. She hated what he and your clubs were doing, said he should spend more time at home with us. They fought about it all the time. She even threatened to leave him if he didn't stop, but my dad wouldn't budge. After that last big rescue of those kids? That's when her paranoia kicked into overdrive. She was convinced you'd all get exposed, and somehow, it would blow back on me as his daughter, and as your girlfriend."

I'm stunned. "You never told me that."

"Shephard made a comment once, when he was drunk, about how my dad might've benefited from her death. I thought he was just rambling. But now it feels like he was telling the truth."

"Fucking hell." I rub my face, trying to make sense of it all. "Why would my men be involved? I trust them."

Nicole looks at me, her voice hollow. "Because they're all tied up in this, Maddox. The vigilante stuff. Maybe my dad held something over their heads. Or maybe they're not as loyal to you as you think."

My mom's face is pale. She's known about the vigilante work for years since my father founded the Zaffre Wolves, and she's known I kept it going after his death. She's had to be ready to cover for me in case anything ever went sideways. But this? This is something none of us could have seen coming.

Nicole could be next. We both know it.

I turn to my mom, desperation in my voice. "We need a place to lay low. Somewhere no one will find us."

She nods, rushing to her room and returning with a set of keys. "Take the Jeep. Head to the family cabin. No one will know you're there."

Nicole and I say quick goodbyes, my mom making me swear to stay safe. As we pull away from the house, the weight of what's coming bears down on me.

This isn't just about revenge anymore. This is survival and we're running out of time.

At the cabin, I park in front of the little house and lead Nicole inside, my eyes constantly flickering around, scanning the tree lined dirt driveway and shadows to ensure we weren't followed. My heart pounds in my chest as the adrenaline from the escape wears off, but I can't let my guard down yet. The house feels eerily quiet, the kind of silence that amplifies every creak and soft thud, making me hyper aware of even the smallest noise.

Once inside, I lock the door behind us and take a deep breath. Nicole watches me with wide eyes, her anxiety written on her face, but I keep mine neutral. I can't let her see the whirlwind of thoughts racing through my head. I pull out my phone and scroll to Jorge's name, dialing quickly. The phone rings only twice before he picks up.

"Hey man, where the fuck you been?" Jorge's voice is casual and cool. It's not unusual for me to go off grid for a day or two, so he doesn't have any reason to be suspicious, not yet at least.

"I need a favor, Jorge," I say, keeping my tone as measured as possible. "And you can't tell a damn soul."

The casualness in his voice shifts immediately, turning serious. "Yeah, okay. What's up?" In the background, I hear the faint sound of work at the shop. It quiets, the sudden silence telling me he's moving somewhere more private.

I glance at Nicole, who's sitting on the couch, arms wrapped around herself, eyes filled with worry. Turning my back slightly, I lower my voice. "I need you to look into Geoffrey's whereabouts. Specifically, in the days leading up to Martha's death. Do it without tipping him off. Then for the day of her death, I need an hour-by-hour breakdown of where he was."

There's a pause on the other end of the line. Jorge knows how serious this is. He's not an idiot. When he speaks again, there's an edge to his voice. "Maddox, what's this about?" He's worried now, and he should be. If Geoffrey was involved, it means this whole thing goes deeper than we thought.

"Just trust me, Jorge," I say, my voice low and firm. "I'll explain everything later, but right now, I need you to get me that information. No questions, no leaks. I'm going dark for a few days, and if anyone asks where I am, tell the guys my mom was hurt in an accident. She'll back it up if necessary." I'm gambling here, praying that he isn't involved. He's my VP, my closest friend, like a true brother. If this leaks, I'll know my whole club is gone and that makes this even worse of a situation.

Another pause, and I can sense him thinking it over. "Okay," he finally says, his tone shifting to resigned determination. "I'll get on it. I'll call you as soon as I know something."

The line goes dead, and I immediately text my mom, crafting a detailed backstory for the accident she needs to fake. I give her instructions to follow precisely if anyone inquires, down to the time, place, and fake injury she'll claim.

With that done, I slip the phone into my pocket and glance at Nicole. She's staring at me, her expression a mixture of fear and hope. "What now?" she asks, her voice shaky.

"Now we lay low," I tell her, sitting beside her on the couch. I can feel her trembling slightly, so I pull her close, feeling the weight of responsibility pressing on my chest. "We wait for Jorge's intel, then we'll know where to go from there."

Nicole rests her head against my shoulder, and I feel her slowly exhale. Even as we sit here in relative safety, my mind is already spinning. If Geoffrey's involved, this is about to get messy. No one in the club is going to see it coming, and it means we're running out of people we can trust. Every second we wait, the danger grows. I have to stay one step ahead, or we're both dead.

The house feels like a temporary shield, but I know it won't last long. Whatever happens next, we have to be ready to fight.

Chapter 8

Nicole

Maddox and I sit side by side at the table, going over the details of my mom's murder, piecing together everything we can, now that more people seem to be involved. His body is close to mine, our arms brushing every so often, and each accidental touch sends a wave of heat through me. I try to focus on the papers in front of me, but it's hard when I can feel his presence like this, protective and determined.

Every time he glances at me for a little too long, my heart flutters in a way I wish it wouldn't. I can't help but remember how fucking sexy he used to look when he was working or deep in thought. The intensity in his eyes, the way his muscles tensed when he strategized. It used to drive me wild, and even now, despite everything, those old feelings are hard to shake.

I hold back. I can't make a move. Not when there's this dark cloud of doubt hanging over us, over him.

The Maddox I knew before would never betray me. The Maddox sitting beside me now? I can't be sure. He says my father locked him up, knocked him out and threw him in that basement, but there's no proof. No one to back up his story except him. The thought that maybe he could've been involved in my mom's death eats at me. The betrayal would be too much, so I try not to think about it. It lingers at the back of my mind like a shadow.

I steal a glance at him as he jots down something in the margins of the timeline we've been working on, his brow furrowed in concentration. It's hard to reconcile the man I'm looking at now with the possibility that he might be hiding something. He's the only solid thing I've ever trusted, the one person I thought I could always count on, but now, nothing is certain.

That thought breaks me a little more inside.

It's already bad enough that my dad is involved. Knowing he had a hand in my mother's death, or at least in covering up whatever happened, has shattered the image I've had of him my entire life. With Shep and Geoffrey possibly involved too, everything is crumbling. None of it makes any fucking sense, and the more we dig, the more twisted it becomes.

I rub my temples, trying to keep my focus on the evidence in front of me, but my mind is spinning. I need answers, real answers, and I need to know who I can truly trust. Most of all, I need to know if Maddox is still the man I fell for all those years ago, or if I've been blind all along.

"You okay?" Maddox asks softly, setting the pen down as he watches me rub my forehead.

"No. Far from it," I mutter, my voice thick with emotion.

He reaches out, his hand hovering over mine, but I flinch back. The flicker of pain that flashes across his face strikes me like a punch to the gut, and I can't bear to look at him any longer. I stand abruptly and walk away, my thoughts spiraling, my chest tightening. What if he brought me here to silence me? What if everything I've trusted, everything I've known is a lie?

My breathing picks up, and I can't stop it. Panic crashes over me like a tidal wave. I grab at my chest, trying to steady myself, gripping the edge of the kitchen counter as if it's the only thing keeping me upright.

Maddox is there, wrapping his arms around me, pulling me into him. His hold is tight, almost desperate. "Shhh," he hums, trying to soothe me. "We'll be okay."

"Will we?" I snap, wrenching myself from his grasp as the tears come, hot and heavy. My voice trembles, but the anger burning inside me gives me the strength to finally say what's been boiling in my gut.

"What's that supposed to mean?" His tone hardens, and he looks at me like I've just slapped him across the face.

"Oh, come on, Maddox," I spit, my words cutting like glass. "You're really going to stand there and tell me that both your men and my father's men are involved in all this, and you had no idea? Do you think I'm that naive? If you're here to shut me up, then just fucking do it already."

His face twists in shock, then in pain, like I've just ripped something from him. "What the hell, Nic? I'd *never* hurt you," he yells, his voice cracking under the weight of my accusations.

"Right," I snap back, my voice full of venom. "Neither would my father. Or Shep. Or your men. But guess what? They did. They're all fucking involved, Maddox. Don't stand there and act like I'm stupid. At least have the guts to admit that I know the truth."

He steps back, his face full of disbelief as he scoffs bitterly. "I can't fucking believe this."

"You kept me under lock and key, just like my dad. You made sure I was too scared, too unsure of myself, to dig into my mom's death. You and him, you both played me. How could you? I loved you. I trusted you." My voice rises with each word, my body trembling with the weight of my heartbreak and anger.

"I was trying to protect you," he shouts, his eyes wild. "I didn't want you to be next. If anything happened to you, it would have killed me, Nicole. So yeah, maybe I pushed too hard. Maybe I fucked up and lost you, but I was never involved in anything to do with your mom's death. Never."

I don't believe him. Not fully. "Sure," I scoff, the challenge heavy in my voice.

Maddox's hands curl into fists, his knuckles white. He stares at me, his chest rising and falling with heavy breaths. Then, with a defeated shake of his head, he throws his hands up, his voice raw. "Fuck, Nic. If you really think I'm involved, if you honestly believe I had anything to do with this, then take the damn Jeep and leave. Go! Get the fuck out of here and find some place where I can't ever find you."

He hurls the keys at me, and they hit the floor with a sharp clatter. He slams his hands down on the counter, his body trembling as he braces himself against it, his head hanging low.

I bend down and pick up the keys, my hand shaking as I grip them tightly. With a deep breath, I cross the room, grabbing the file and shoving it into my purse as pages fold, my heart pounding in my chest. Slinging the bag over my shoulder, I head toward the door, my mind racing, trying to make sense of everything.

As soon as I step outside, the world explodes. Gunfire rips through the air, and the wood railing beside me splinters. I barely register what's happening before instinct takes over. I duck down, pressing myself against the steps as bullets whiz past, my breath catching in my throat.

Before I can even process the chaos, Maddox bursts out the door, his eyes wild and frantic. More gunshots ring out, forcing him to yank me back inside. His grip on my arm is tight, almost painful, as he pulls me through the house, both of us ducking low, trying to avoid the deadly barrage.

"We've got to go," he mutters, pulling me toward the back door. His movements are quick and calculated, as if he's done this a hundred times before. He peers outside, scanning the area, then pulls me out, keeping us low as we sprint around to the Jeep. My heart is in my throat, each breath coming in short, panicked gasps.

Somehow, he's taken the keys from me. Before I can even ask how, we're in the Jeep with him in the driver's seat, me trembling in the passenger side. The gunshots are still ringing in the distance as the vehicle lurches forward, and he speeds down a narrow trail, trees scraping violently against the sides of the Jeep.

"Did you get hit?" he asks, his voice tight as he grips the steering wheel, navigating us through the thick woods. His eyes flicker between the road and me, filled with worry and something more desperate.

"No," I manage to choke out, tears spilling down my cheeks.

"I need you to call Jorge from my phone," he says, his voice strained as he hands me the device. "Tell him we're headed toward Tuscan to the meet place. He'll know what I'm talking about."

I hesitate, my fingers hovering over the phone. "What if he tracked your call?" I ask, my voice shaking. "What if Jorge is the reason someone knew we were here?"

The gunfire has stopped, and the adrenaline is fading, but the fear still grips me tightly. Reaching out to the person who might have betrayed us feels like walking into a trap. It's reckless. It's stupid.

"Trust me, Nic. Please," Maddox pleads, his voice raw.

Reluctantly, I dial the number and relay the message, my voice breaking as I speak. Jorge is calm on the other end, promising to meet us. When I hang up, the doubt gnaws at me, twisting in my gut. I wipe the tears from my face, trying to breathe, trying to hold it together.

Maddox suddenly veers onto the highway, the Jeep bouncing as he takes the exit in the opposite direction of Tuscan. My stomach flips as I grip the seat.

"Where are we going?" I ask, my voice thin, full of uncertainty.

Maddox's jaw tightens, his knuckles white against the steering wheel. "We're about to see if Jorge is a rat," he mutters.

My heart skips a beat. "How?"

"We're going to see if my men are at the shop or if they're already on their way to take us out," he explains, his voice low and grim. "If they're still at the shop, then Jorge didn't tell them. If they're not…" He pauses, his eyes hardening. "Well, that really fucking sucks."

A cold shiver runs down my spine. The air between us feels heavy with dread, the weight of betrayal looming over us. I can only pray Maddox is right, because if he's not, then everything is about to come crashing down.

Maddox tightens his grip on the wheel, his voice low but edged with frustration. "Also, whoever was firing has shit aim. A professional would've hit you the first time. You were wide open. The entire time after, they couldn't strike us while moving. It's not our men back there."

His words hang heavy in the air, the implications sinking in. My pulse quickens, and I glance out the window, my mind racing.

"So what?" I say, forcing the question out despite the lump forming in my throat. "They hired someone to come kill us?"

Maddox exhales sharply through his nose, his eyes narrowed in thought. "It makes no sense. They could've taken us out if they really wanted to. Hell, they'd want us dead just to cover their tracks and twist the narrative. Something isn't right." His knuckles whiten as he grips the wheel tighter, driving us towards town.

The miles stretch on, the tension between us thick. Every minute feels like a lifetime, and yet, the pieces of this twisted puzzle remain elusive. After a bit, we roll slowly past his shop. The lot is full, his men working as usual, none of them the wiser to what's unraveling behind the scenes. But Jorge is nowhere to be seen.

Maddox picks up his phone and dials, his voice steely. "You there yet?" he asks when Jorge picks up.

"About five minutes out, boss," Jorge replies, his voice casual. Maddox's eyes darken as he turns to me, putting the call on speaker.

"Well, I hate to do this to you," Maddox says, voice tense. "But go back. I'm not coming."

There's a brief silence on the other end, and I can hear the worry creep into Jorge's voice. "What's going on, Maddox?"

Maddox's expression hardens, his words clipped. "Someone tried to kill Nicole and me. We barely got away. We've got a rat, and I had to make sure it wasn't you."

The line goes quiet for a beat, and then Jorge responds, his tone heavy with concern. "It's not me, man. You think Geoffrey's the one?"

Maddox's eyes flick to the shop as we drive past, watching Geoffrey move between the workers. "Yeah. Possibly."

"I left him at the shop," Jorge says, confirming what we see. "What do you want me to do?"

"Did you get the info I wanted?" Maddox asks, shifting gears and driving off.

"Maybe," Jorge hesitates, "but it looks clean. He was at work the day Martha was killed. Stayed late, left after the shooting. The month leading up to it, nothing suspicious. His usual routine of work and clubs. Nothing out of the ordinary."

Maddox's jaw clenches. "What about him being in the same places as Martha? Any overlap?"

"No, boss. He didn't miss work. If anything, the guy's like clockwork. He doesn't stray."

Maddox falls silent for a moment, processing. Then, his voice hardens further. "I need you to do something else."

"Name it, boss."

"I need to know who was firing at us out at my parents' cabin," Maddox says, the weight of the request heavy in his voice.

Jorge doesn't hesitate. "I'll find out. Be safe, man."

"Yup," Maddox says, and hangs up, tossing the phone aside as we hit the interstate. He doesn't tell me where we're going. I don't ask. I just sit there, staring out the window, trying to make sense of the chaos around us.

Chapter 9

Maddox

I pull into a small, out-of-the-way hotel just off the highway, the kind of place where no one would think to look for us. I park the Jeep in the back, slipping it between two trucks and backing it in deep to make sure it's hard to spot but with an easy exit if we need it. The thought of being found, of whoever came for us earlier tracking us here, sends a ripple of tension through my body, but I shake it off. We're four hours from Phoenix, far enough that we should be able to rest and game plan.

At the front desk, I book a room for two nights, paying in cash under a false name. We don't need any more digital footprints than we already have. I make sure to request a room on the ground floor, near an exit, just in case we need to get out fast.

Inside, Nicole wastes no time heading to the bathroom, peeling off the clothes she's been wearing for hours. She's still jittery from the close call earlier, but she's trying to hide it. I can tell. She grabs a set of fresh clothes we picked up on the way, disappearing behind the door to wash off the dirt and fear from the day. The sound of the shower running is almost a relief, a moment of normalcy in the middle of this shit storm.

While she's in there, Jorge calls. The moment I hear his heavy breathing, I know he's on edge. "Maddox," he pants. "I'm at the cabin now. Whoever was firing at you was using an M240. High caliber. Long range automatic fire, man. They were positioned up on a hill off the road, so there's only one possible shooter." He pauses, like he's gathering his thoughts. "There's a set of tire tracks and footprints up there. I sent photographs to Aiden to see if we can get a hit on the vehicle. Might help us figure out who the hell this was."

I rub the back of my neck, tension building. "What about the cabin's camera system?"

"I'm working on that now. The cameras caught some movement in the distance, but the system's old. It's too blurry to get a clear visual. I'm downloading the footage and sending it to Aiden as well. He might be able to clean it up, but don't expect miracles."

"Good," I reply, feeling that knot in my chest loosen just slightly. "Keep me updated."

"Of course, boss. I'll get back to you once I have something solid."

Aiden is a trusty source. One we use to do some dirty, behind the scenes digging when needed. It'll cost a pretty penny, but when it comes to keeping Nicole safe, she's fucking worth it.

We hang up, and the room falls into a strange, heavy silence. That uneasy feeling from earlier creeps back, the kind that makes you hyper aware of every little noise. I let out a slow breath, turning around just as Nicole steps out of the bathroom.

She's standing there in the doorway, her hair still damp, dressed in the new clothes, a loose shirt and jeans that hug her body in all the right ways without being too tight. Her eyes meet mine, and I can see the worry in them.

There's still that distance between us, the one she's been holding onto since everything fell apart. This moment feels different. She's looking at me like she wants answers, real answers, like she's searching for something she's afraid to find.

"You weren't involved in any of it?" she asks, her voice soft but heavy with doubt.

I close the distance between us in two steps, standing right in front of her. My eyes bore into hers, and I can see her searching my face for any sign of deception. "No, Nic. I wasn't."

The tension between us breaks like a dam, and suddenly her arms are around me, clinging to me like I'm her lifeline. I wrap my arms around her, pulling her in close, my chin resting on top of her head. For the first time today, I feel a rush of relief. She didn't get hurt. She's here, in my arms safe. At least for now.

"I'm sorry," she whispers, her voice muffled against my chest. "I'm sorry I accused you earlier."

I hold her tighter, speaking softly into her hair. "I couldn't hurt you, Nicole. I love you too much to ever think of doing anything that would put you in harm's way. I wish I'd made you see that while we were still together." My words are raw, unguarded, spilling out because it feels like this could be the last time we ever get to say them. We're being hunted and without knowing who, and because I don't believe it's our men, we don't have the upper hand.

Nicole looks up at me, her big, tear-filled eyes locking onto mine. The intensity between us deepens. It's like the space between us shrinks to nothing. The way she's looking at me now, it's almost like she wants to close the gap, to forget everything for a moment. I can see it in her eyes, the way her lips part ever so slightly. And fuck, the way she's making me feel right now, it's driving me wild.

My body reacts before my mind can catch up. All I want is to make up for the lost time, to feel her against me in every way. To erase the pain we caused each other. My pulse quickens as the urge to close the gap, to take her right here, grows almost unbearable.

"What happens if we don't win this?" she asks, her voice barely above a whisper, but before I can even begin to answer, her phone lights up. The sudden ring pierces the silence like a gunshot.

"It's my dad," she says, her voice edged with uncertainty.

I lock eyes with her, every instinct in me flaring up. "Answer it on speaker. Tell him you went on a girls' trip if he asks. Say it's to clear your mind."

She nods, her fingers fumbling for just a second before she puts it on speaker. "Hey, Dad," she greets him, her voice calm, masking the feel of betrayal brewing beneath her flustered exterior.

"Listen to me, Nic. Are you alone?" His voice is tight, controlled, but there's an urgency in it that sets off alarms in my head.

Nicole glances at me, and I give her a quick nod. She's sharp, she knows how to play this. "Give me a sec." She closes the bathroom door behind her, making it sound like she's stepping away from a group of friends. "I'm alone now," she says. "Did you get in touch with Maddox?"

Her dad's next words send a chill crawling down my spine. "No, and we have bigger problems. If you get in touch with him, don't leave his side. Don't come to my house, and wherever you are, don't go home."

My stomach twists painfully. He's warning her to stay with me, not away from me, which makes no sense if he was involved in any of this. He should want her as far away from me as possible. Something is off, something big.

Nicole's voice cracks as she asks, "What's going on, Dad?" Her tears sound so real that even I can't tell if she's acting or if this is raw emotion pouring out of her.

Her father's voice comes back, thick with a mix of fear and regret. "There are things I never told you. Maddox doesn't even know. Only Shephard does. The people who killed your mom have been blackmailing me for years. They've threatened to kill you if you ever got too close to the truth. That's why Shephard was trying to steer you away from digging into your mom's death. They know, Nicole. They know you're involved now and they're coming for you... and Maddox."

I feel a cold, heavy weight settle in my gut. Nicole looks up at me, her eyes wide with shock. I take the phone from her, gripping it hard, my voice low and dangerous. "Who are they?"

Her father audibly gasps, his surprise clear. "Maddox? Jesus, I'm glad you're okay. I thought they got to you when you disappeared."

"Who. Are. They?" I repeat, my patience thinning.

Brickton takes a breath, his voice steadying. "They go by The Vipers. They're a club out of Ohio. A group that's been systematically taking down powerful clubs across the country. They approached me months before Martha's death, wanting to take over my club. I refused. To make an example out of me, they killed her. I thought I could protect your club by keeping it quiet, by keeping you in the dark, but I was wrong. They bugged everything, Maddox. My place, yours, and when Nicole came to you asking for help, they heard everything."

My blood boils as his words sink in. "And now they're after us."

"Yeah," he says, voice heavy. "Are you safe right now?"

I look over at Nicole. She's pale but standing strong. "We're safe."

"You don't let anything happen to my daughter, Maddox."

My jaw clenches. "They'll have to go through me first, Brickton. I'll die before I let anyone harm her. You have my word."

There's a beat of silence before his voice drops to a grave whisper. "One last thing, Maddox. Weep the dead."

My chest tightens. The coded phrase hits me like a punch to the gut. I grunt in acknowledgment, my mind racing as I hang up the call. Weep the dead. It's a signal, a message meant only for me. A clue to the next move.

Everything just shifted again, the weight of the truth sinking in deeper. This time, I have an advantage. The game is changing, and I'm no longer playing defense.

Chapter 10

Nicole

"Weep the dead?" I ask Maddox, my voice barely above a whisper.

He strides over to the desk, scribbling down a frantic series of words and numbers that look like a foreign language to me. My heart races as I try to decipher his urgency.

"What does it mean?"

He doesn't look up, lost in his frantic writing. I can feel a weight settling in my stomach as I watch him slip back into his shoes and grab the Jeep keys.

"It's a code," he says, his tone clipped.

"For what?" I press, desperate for answers, but his gaze hardens.

"Shhh," he replies, the command sharp. He turns to the door, his body tense, instincts kicking in. "Get in the bathroom, lock the door, and don't make a sound."

My heart races as I comply, darting into the bathroom. I lock the door behind me and sink down into the tub, pulling the curtain closed. It's flimsy protection, but it feels like a barrier between me and whatever is about to happen.

As I sit there, the silence is deafening. Out of nowhere, a loud barrage of gunfire erupts from the other room, sending a shockwave of fear through me. I duck down instinctively, flattening myself in the tub, arms wrapped around my head as bullets slam into the wall, plaster raining down like confetti.

The sound of chaos fills the air, but I stifle my scream, forcing myself to remain quiet. Maddox knew something was coming; he must have a plan.

The gunfire abruptly ceases, replaced by the slam of the hotel door slamming open, then the sound of male voices, their tones low and menacing.

"They came in here and didn't leave. The Jeep is still out back," one of them says, voice dripping with malice.

The bathroom door handle rattles, sending a surge of adrenaline coursing through me. I hold my breath, frozen in place. There's a gunshot, and the handle clatters to the floor, the door swinging open violently.

I barely have time to lift my head before two men, clad in all black, rip the curtain open, their eyes locking onto me.

"Ahh, there's the daughter," the blonde man sneers in a rough accent, his grip like iron as he yanks me up by my upper arm.

I scream, fear coursing through my veins. I can't hear Maddox, and the thought that he might be dead sends a fresh wave of panic crashing over me.

"Where's your boyfriend?" the other man demands, his gaze piercing.

I stare back defiantly. "He went for supper," I lie, desperation fueling my words because Maddox isn't dead if they're asking about his whereabouts.

"Try again. Jeep is outside," he retorts, eyes narrowing in suspicion.

"He walked to avoid drawing attention," I insist, my heart racing.

The men exchange glances, suspicion mounting. Then they pull me roughly into the hotel room, scanning the surroundings. My heart pounds as I try to gauge the situation, looking for any sign of Maddox.

"Dear ole daddy was naughty. He called and gave us up. He knows that is wrong. Now tell me, how did your man go for food if he was just on the phone?" The brown-haired man's voice drips with mockery as he brushes his fingers down my cheek, a cold shiver racing down my spine.

"He left right after," I reply, maintaining my composure.

"Wrong. We were already outside watching the room," he sneers.

I shrug, my heart thudding in my chest as the blonde man raises his hand, ready to strike. Before he can move, a sudden grunt erupts from him, and blood dribbles from his mouth as he releases his grip on me.

Maddox emerges from the shadows; fury etched across his face. Time seems to slow as I watch him move, every muscle coiled, ready for action.

In a fluid motion, he ducks beneath the other man's wild swing and counters with a powerful knee to the man's groin. The impact sends the man staggering back, and I can't help but feel a rush of relief mixed with awe as Maddox takes control.

The man recovers quickly, eyes blazing with fury as he swings at Maddox, a wild punch that Maddox narrowly dodges. The air between them crackles with intensity. Maddox retaliates with a hard right hook, connecting with the guy's jaw with a sickening crack. The man shakes it off like it's nothing, coming back with a vengeance.

Their fists collide in a brutal exchange, one hit after another, flesh meeting flesh with a resounding impact. It's like watching a fight scene from an action movie. Each punch is sharp, calculated, but fueled by raw emotion. Maddox's knuckles are already bloodied, and the guy's face is swelling, but neither of them gives in. They're locked in a relentless, primal battle for dominance.

I stand frozen, my heart pounding as I watch Maddox absorb a crushing blow to the ribs, his body jolting, but he doesn't falter. He swings back with an uppercut, sending the man stumbling back for just a moment before they're at it again, fists flying, sweat and blood mingling in the heat of the fight.

Every movement is brutal and precise, the sound of each impact echoing in the space like thunder. The tension is suffocating, each moment stretched out as they battle for control, both refusing to go down. It's raw, savage, and terrifyingly mesmerizing to witness.

Before I can fully process what's happening next, Maddox lunges for the knife sticking out of the blonde man on the floor, still slick with blood, yanking it from the man's back with a swift, decisive motion. With precision, he drives it into the throat of the brown-haired man, who gasps, eyes wide in shock.

Blood spills like a crimson waterfall as Maddox twists the blade, ripping it sideways, opening the man's jugular. The grotesque reality of it all crashes over me, but there's no time to process. I'm paralyzed in both horror and admiration.

The brown-haired man's gurgled cries fill the air, but Maddox doesn't relent, his expression a mix of rage and determination.

Just as quickly as it began, the fight is over, and I'm yanked from the chaos. Maddox pulls me out of the hotel toward the Jeep, cruciality fueling his every move, and as we speed away from the scene, adrenaline surges through my veins. My heart races not only from the fear but also from the realization that our fight is just beginning.

We pull up hours later to a graveyard overrun with wild grass and tangled weeds, the air thick with the scent of damp earth and decay. It's clear this place has been neglected, a forgotten corner of the world with few visitors. As I step out of the Jeep, my gaze is immediately drawn to the sea of motorcycles parked in the lot, their chrome glinting in the sun, a contrast to the somber backdrop. Some belong to my father's men, some are Maddox's.

My heart races when I spot my father standing just past the entrance, his posture tense yet relieved. I take off running, my shoes pounding against the gravel, and slam into him, wrapping my arms tightly around him. The weight of the world falls away for a moment as we hug, the closeness of his presence anchoring me through the chaos.

As I pull back, I see the men surrounding us, several armed and vigilant, their eyes scanning the area for any signs of trouble. The atmosphere is thick with tension, the air heavy with unspoken fears and impending violence. My dad and Maddox are deep in conversation, their brows furrowed, strategizing about what comes next.

"They keep finding us," Maddox says, his voice low and gravelly. "I think you're right, our phones are bugged, so I tossed them on the way here, leading them in the other direction before swinging back this way." The memory of tossing my phone out the window flashes in my mind, his fierce determination etched into my memory. He promised me he'd buy me any phone I wanted after this nightmare is over.

"We all left our phones behind as well," my dad adds, adjusting himself on a sun-drenched bench, the light catching the lines of worry etched on his face. "All bikes are clear of trackers."

"Good. Now, tell me everything you know about these fuckers." Maddox's voice shifts, taking on a commanding tone that brooks no argument. He's a force of nature, a whirlwind of anger and readiness for blood.

These types of meetings used to wind him up and afterwards, he'd come home to me, and we'd fuck with him getting his anger and energy out. Of course, I didn't realize the true intentions of the meetings but now I see why he would be so wound up afterwards. I can't help but feel a pang of jealousy and sadness at the thought of him with someone else to relieve his stress this last year, even though I was the one who ended things between us. The past few days spent in close quarters have reignited feelings I thought I'd buried.

"They're slowly taking over multiple towns across the country," my dad explains, his expression grim. "They have men everywhere. Half of the clubs they've taken were either forcibly converted or had their members eliminated before being claimed and renamed."

"Everyone has a weakness. What's theirs?" Jorge interjects, the cigarette between his lips swaying with his words, a nonchalant facade masking the underlying tension.

Just then, Shepherd walks over. Upon seeing me, he offers a tight-lipped smile that doesn't quite reach his eyes. I stand and move toward him, wrapping my arms around him in a hug that feels both familiar and fragile.

"I'm so sorry I scared you, Nicole," he murmurs, his voice low and filled with sincerity. "I just needed you to lay off without telling you why. Of course, you're stubborn like your old man."

With teary eyes, I cling to him. "You're forgiven, Shep."

He pats my back gently, his warmth comforting as he walks me back to the group. He kneels beside my dad, and I slip back into my seat next to Maddox, who watches me with a guarded expression, a horde of emotions swirling behind his eyes.

"Looks like they have their own rats," Shepherd continues, a serious note entering his tone. "They've made some enemies, taking over other clubs, murdering their women and children. They're currently holed up at a rental house with only six men at the moment. Well, four now that Maddox took out two." He nods toward Maddox, who reaches over and shakes his hand.

"Did they take the bait?" Maddox asks, his voice steady yet tinged with urgency. I cock my head, trying to grasp the gravity of their words.

"The note you left that made no sense?" I ask.

"MC lingo for coordinates," he answers me.

"Yup, they deciphered that note quickly. They're currently heading back to the cabin where a dear friend is about to greet them. Their president, though, he's not here. He's calling the shots from back home," Shepherd says.

"Fuck," my dad curses under his breath, the tension in the air palpable.

I watch as Maddox's jaw tightens, determination radiating off him. The stakes have never been higher, and as I sit among the men who have become my reluctant family, I can't shake the feeling that we are on the brink of something explosive. Each word exchanged, every plan laid out, feels like a step toward an inevitable confrontation. I brace myself, ready to face whatever comes next, because I know one thing for sure, we're in this fight together, and there's no turning back.

As I sit and listen to them strategize about how to draw the leader out, a weight lifts off my shoulders. Knowing the truth about my mom's death brings me a sense of relief I didn't think possible. It feels good to realize that the men around me aren't the traitors I once suspected, and that my father had no part in her murder.

Geoffrey approaches from where he had been standing, extending his hand toward

Maddox. Maddox stands to meet him, pulling him into a firm embrace.

"Sorry I ever doubted you," Maddox admits, sincerity lacing his words.

Geoffrey waves his hand dismissively. "Eh, it's all good. We're past that now."

My attention snaps back to my father as he speaks. "So, we're doing this?"

The question hangs heavy in the air, and the men from both motorcycle clubs begin to nod in agreement, a shared understanding settling among them.

I let out a breath, the gravity of the situation crashing down on me. Something tells me that this plan is going to escalate quickly, and I brace myself for the storm that's about to break.

A week later, I find myself at my house with Maddox, the remnants of our chaotic week now softened by the warmth of this moment. We've returned the Jeep to his mother, the vehicle fixed up as best as it could be after our harrowing escape. Now, we're cozied up on the couch, a blanket draped over us, the remnants of supper lingering in the air, takeout that was delivered and devoured in comfortable silence.

He's spent every moment with me, wrapping me in his presence like a warm blanket. I find myself at his job, lingering in the corners of the bustling shop, a comforting routine that allows him to keep an eye on me while he works.

There's a sense of safety in being near him again, in the way he glances my way, his eyes filled with a mixture of protectiveness and something deeper. Beneath that comfort lies a nagging ache in my chest, a constant reminder that the intimacy we once shared has transformed. We're not the same as we were before my mother's death, and that reality weighs heavily on me.

Every laugh we share feels tinged with a bittersweet nostalgia, each moment colored by the distance that's grown between us. The way he brushes his fingers against mine sometimes sends a shiver down my spine, igniting old sparks, yet I can feel the walls we've built still standing tall between us. I want to reach out, to bridge that gap, but fear holds me back. Fear of what it might mean if we tried to reclaim what we lost.

It's a strange mix of comfort and longing, being close yet feeling so far away. I catch myself stealing glances at him, trying to memorize the way the light catches in his hair, how his lips curve into a smile that still makes my heart race. Each moment reminds me of what we once had, what we've lost, and I can't shake the feeling that despite our proximity, we're both walking on the edge of something fragile and uncertain.

Maddox shifts slightly, pulling me closer, the warmth of his body seeping into me. I let him hold me, not knowing how many more chances we'll get after today.

"Would you ever give me a second chance?" he asks, his voice low and sincere, almost like he could read the thoughts flowing through my mind.

I lay my head on his chest, the rhythm of his heartbeat soothing me. "I've been waiting for you to ask that."

He glances down at me, his expression shifting from curiosity to hope. "Yeah?" His lips curl into a smile, the kind that lights up his eyes.

"Yes. I think after everything we've been through the last couple of weeks, I've realized I was wrong to dump you."

"I was a bit of an asshole to you," he admits, his voice tinged with regret.

"Yeah, but I should've seen why. I was so focused on myself that I didn't recognize you were protecting me in your own way."

With a soft smile, he lays me back on the couch, settling over me. "I'd like to make it all up to you, Nicole. Start fresh."

"How?" I whisper, the anticipation hanging thick in the air.

He leans down and kisses me, igniting every spark I've ever felt for him over the last decade of knowing each other. It's like a firework igniting in the pit of my stomach, a rush of warmth enveloping me. I grip his hair, pulling him closer, and wrap my legs around his waist, our bodies fitting together perfectly.

"Damn baby," he breathes, rocking his hips against me. I can feel his erection pressing into me, heat pooling low in my belly.

"Fuck me like it's the last time you'll ever get to," I breathe, emotion thickening my voice.

The uncertainty of tomorrow hangs over us, and I want to etch this moment into my memory, to always remember how it feels to have him deep inside me.

"You want me to fuck you hard? To claim you as mine once again? To fill you so full you're leaking and covered in my fucking come, baby?" His voice is low and gravelly, sending shivers down my spine as he nips at my earlobe, trailing his lips down my neck, over my collarbone.

"Yes, Maddox. Make me regret ever leaving you."

With a determined gleam in his eyes, he sits up, his hands deftly stripping my clothes off. I fumble with his jeans, eager to feel him against me. He tears his clothes away, urgency electrifying the air around us, and then he sits back on the couch, pulling me onto his lap.

I straddle him, my wetness gliding over his hard cock, teasing both of us as I rub myself against him. The heat of his desire radiates through me, mingling with my own. My hands roam over his defined chest, feeling every muscle tense under my touch, desperate to memorize each ridge, each curve. His body is a landscape I've traveled before, but it's been too long, and now every inch feels new.

Maddox grips my hips hard, his fingers digging into my flesh as he growls, "you're driving me crazy, Nic. Quit teasing." With one swift motion, he slams me down onto his cock, filling me completely in a single thrust. The sensation is overwhelming, and a scream of pleasure rips from my throat, echoing in the still room. "Fuck, you feel so tight," he groans, thrusting upward as I rise on my knees, only to drop back down, taking him deep again. My body responds instinctively, grinding down onto him, matching his rhythm, fucking him just how I know he likes.

"Get on your feet, Nic," he orders, his voice dripping with command. I obey instantly, lifting myself onto my feet as he grips my ass and guides me up and down his cock. Each bounce sends waves of pleasure through me, my thighs trembling with the effort. "That's it, baby," he growls, his hands gripping me tighter. "Fuck yourself on my dick. Soak it. Make a mess on me."

His words push me closer to the edge. "You want me to come all over your cock?" I gasp, slamming down harder, my body shaking with the building pressure inside me.

"Fuck yes. Cover my dick with that sweet pussy, Nic. I want to feel you dripping all over me." His eyes lock onto mine, possessive and hungry. "This cunt is mine. You hear me? All fucking mine."

"Yes!" I scream as the orgasm crashes through me, my walls squeezing him tight. My body shakes, my nails dig into his chest, and the room spins as I ride out every wave of pleasure.

"Fuck, baby, you're squeezing me so damn tight," he grunts, thrusting up into me even harder, determined to draw every ounce of pleasure from my body.

"I love your dirty mouth," I moan, grinding against him, drawing it out, pushing us both to the brink again. His cock throbs inside me, relentless, claiming every inch of me.

"You know what else you love?" he breathes out huskily, his voice a deep growl that sends shivers down my spine.

"What?" I whisper, desperate for whatever he's about to give me.

"You love when I fill this cunt with my cum. You love being stuffed so full you're leaking." His hips thrust up hard, his cock pulsing as he gets closer. "I'm going to fuck you so deep, Nic, you'll feel me inside you for days."

His words send me over the edge again, another orgasm tearing through me as I scream out his name. "Fuck, Maddox."

"That's it, baby," he growls, his grip on my hips bruising as he slams me down one last time, his warmth spilling inside me. I take all of him, grinding down until there's nothing left to give, my body trembling as he fills me to the brim.

"I'm not finished with you," he whispers darkly, lifting me off his cock. Our combined mess drips down, coating his length as I slide to my knees, eager to finish what he started. I take him into my mouth, my lips wrapping around his thick cock, tasting both of us as I suck him clean.

"Fuck, baby, that mouth of yours," he groans, his hands gripping my hair, guiding my head as I bob up and down, my tongue swirling around his tip, taking him as deep as I can. His cock twitches in my mouth, still sensitive, but I know he loves the feeling of being sucked clean after fucking me raw.

I glance up at him, locking eyes as I suck him harder, making sure he knows I belong to him. His face twists in pleasure, and when I feel him tug my hair harder, I know he's close again.

"On your hands and knees," he growls. I obey without hesitation getting into position on the floor, arching my back as I feel his cock press against my entrance once more. "You're mine, Nic. You're my dirty fucking whore, aren't you?"

"Yes," I moan, my voice thick with lust. "I'm your dirty whore, Maddox. Fuck me like I belong to you."

He slams into me from behind, filling me again with a brutal thrust. His hips rock back and forth, the sound of skin slapping against skin filling the room as he fucks me harder and deeper. Each thrust sends a jolt of pleasure through me, and I can barely breathe from how good it feels.

"Who does this tight pussy belong to?" he grunts, his fingers sliding down to rub my clit as he pounds into me.

"You," I scream, barely able to hold myself up as he drives me wild. "It's yours, Maddox."

"Damn right it is," he growls. "And I'm going to fill this tight ass too. You want that, Nic? Want me to fuck your ass and fill you there too?"

"Yes," I cry out, desperate for more. He pulls out and with one quick motion, slides into my ass, groaning as I scream from the intense pleasure.

"Fuck, you feel so tight back here, baby," he groans, slamming into me repeatedly, his hand gripping my hip as he takes me completely. "You're my filthy little slut, aren't you?"

"Yes Maddox, I'm yours," I moan, the pleasure and pain mixing as he fucks me harder, his fingers sliding into my pussy, making me scream as he finger fucks me until our mixed release drips out of me.

He pulls his fingers out, his hand coated and full of cum. He reaches around and wipes it across my chest, coating me in our mess, rubbing it all over my skin.

"I'm going to cover you in my cum, Nic. You're going to be dripping with it while covered in it."

He thrusts into me again, deeper, faster, and with a final growl, I feel him explode inside me, his warmth filling every inch of my ass. His hand squeezes my skin as he rides out his orgasm, leaving me trembling beneath him, completely his.

When he pulls out, we stand after gathering our composure, and he looks down at me with a satisfied smile, watching as his cum drips from both of my holes and down my thigh while my chest is coated. "Fuck, you look so good covered in my cum."

I smile up at him, breathless, still riding the high of what just happened. "I'm yours, Maddox," I whisper, gripping his cock and stroke as his legs shake as his length twitches in my hand. "Always yours."

He leans in, his tongue tracing a slow path from my breasts up to my neck, tasting our combined release he spread across my flesh. His breath is warm against my skin as he whispers, "I missed you like this," his eyes heavy with satisfaction and something deeper.

I smirk, catching my breath, and tease him, "I missed your filthy mouth," laughing softly as I take his hand and lead him to the bathroom.

Under the shower's warm spray, our hands roam each other's bodies, exploring familiar curves and lines, reconnecting through touch. The water cascades down, washing away the tension of the night. By the time we're done, my body is spent, exhaustion settling in with a heavy ache.

We stumble into my bed, the one we used to share, falling into a tangle of limbs. His arms wrap around me, pulling me close, and we drift off, wrapped in the warmth of each other, the past and present blending into a comfortable, intimate mess.

Chapter 11

Maddox

Movement on the bed stirs me awake, and when I open my eyes, I'm greeted by the sight of Nicole, still wrapped in a sheet, passed out with her breasts exposed, her lips slightly parted as she sleeps. The soft morning light casts a glow on her, making her look almost angelic, if angels came with the memories of last night's mind-blowing sex.

I drape an arm over her, pulling her close and pressing a gentle kiss to her lips. "Hmm," she murmurs, stirring softly.

"Shhh," I whisper, closing my eyes again, savoring the feel of her warm body against mine. It wasn't a dream last night, I had her wrapped around me, just like old times, tangled in a mix of raw need that I'd almost forgotten.

Fuck. If Brickton knew the things I've done to his daughter, he'd probably castrate me on the spot and leave me to bleed out.

"Maddox?" Nicole's voice breaks through the silence, soft and sweet, as she drapes an arm over my chest, her fingers lazily tracing the lines of my muscles.

"Yeah, baby?" I reply, opening an eye and brushing a strand of hair from her face.

"Do you still love me?" Her question is so simple, but it hits me with the weight of everything we've been through.

I can't help but smile because the answer comes easily. "I never stopped loving you."

She giggles softly, the sound light and full of relief. I can almost feel her smile, even with my eyes half closed. It's like we're back in the rhythm of things, the way we used to be.

A little while later, we're in the kitchen, falling into our old habit of her making coffee, me whipping up a quick breakfast.

I turn to grab the plates, nearly bumping into her. We do this little dance around each other, laughing quietly, moving in sync like no time has passed. Breakfast is eaten in comfortable silence; the only sounds are the clink of forks on plates and the occasional sip of coffee.

The peace doesn't last long though. Soon enough, we're at the warehouse, where a handful of Brickton's men are staying back to protect Nicole. I pull her close, pressing a kiss to her forehead as she grips my arms tightly.

"Be careful Maddox. Please." Her voice is soft, almost pleading. "Don't let last night be the last time we're together again."

I can see her dad shifting uncomfortably nearby, and Shepherd's cheeks flush slightly. Damn this girl, making this so public. I smile and lean down to kiss her again. "I promise, baby. Then I'm packing my shit and moving back into *my* house."

She arches a brow, teasing me. "Guess I'll have to make you another key since I tossed yours in the river after we broke up."

I shake my head, giving her a final kiss before stepping back. "Smartass," I mutter, smiling as I turn to head out with Brickton and the rest of our crew.

On our bikes, we rumble out of town, the sound of the engines filling the air like a war cry. We're headed to finish this, once and for all. The leader of The Vipers is in town, and today, his reign ends. It's not just about revenge; it's about taking back control for everyone he's hurt, for the lives he's wrecked. For Brickton, it's about getting justice for his wife, whose life ended far too early at their hands.

We dismount our bikes on the side of the road, looking down the hillside at a decrepit building where the intel says he's holed up. Brickton's eyes are cold and focused. He's waited a long time for this.

"You ready?" he asks, looking over at me, his voice steady but filled with the weight of what's coming.

I glance toward the shack of an old business, seeing the faint glint of their bikes parked inside, trying to hide in plain sight. They don't realize who they're dealing with. We're not feared for nothing. Every fight we've been in, we've come out on top and today will be no different.

We sit back, binoculars in hand, scanning inside the shack. The wait is tense, the air thick with anticipation. Finally, through the lens, we spot Calvin Mishol, their leader. He's barely visible, flanked by his men, but it's him, no doubt. The bastard we've been waiting for.

"Count of three, Wolves," I call to my men, raising my gun. They follow suit, ready, waiting for the signal. Brickton mirrors my movements with his crew, the Black Shadows.

The moment hangs in the air, thick with tension.

"Three, two, one."

Gunfire erupts, the sound shattering the quiet as bullets rip into the building. Men pour out, scrambling to return fire, but they don't stand a chance with where we are firing from. We drop them one by one, our aim steady, our focus unwavering. This is what we do.

I raise my hand to halt the firing, Brickton doing the same. The silence that follows is deafening, broken only by the distant crackle of a fire starting in the wreckage. Then, with a loud *boom*, the shack explodes, sending bikes and debris flying as flames consume everything.

"Fuck yeah," Jorge yells, his voice full of triumph.

"Good riddance," Shepherd mutters, spitting on the ground.

We wait, watching for any sign of movement, but no one comes out of the wreckage. When it's clear they're all dead, we head down the slope on foot, making our way around the burning remains of the building.

Satisfied with the carnage, we head back to our bikes, the roar of engines filling the air once again. As we ride back in one formation, the rumble of our bikes is a declaration to everyone around. We're in charge, and we don't fucking lose.

We ride halfway back to the warehouse when something seems off. Up ahead, a roadblock of trucks forms an ominous barricade, and in front of it, men with guns. We slow to a stop, not getting too close, instantly aware that this is no coincidence.

I glance over at Brickton. His jaw tightens, and I know he can sense it too. We've been ambushed. But how? We took out the leader of The Vipers. So, who's running this damn show?

A man steps forward from the line of armed men, his voice cutting through the tension. "Shadows? Wolves? Have your leaders come forward, will you?"

I kick out my stand and swing my leg over my bike, Brickton walking beside me. Our seconds, flanking us, tense for the worst.

"You made quite an announcement earlier," the man continues, grinning like he's got us exactly where he wants us. "It was... explosive." His reddish-brown hair is a sorry excuse for a bowl cut, making him look more like a clown than an MC leader.

"Who the fuck are you?" I ask, voice low and dangerous.

He smirks. "You can call me T for Traitor. Or maybe B for Backstabber. R for Rat works too, if you like."

"What?" Brickton snarls, fists clenched, but the man doesn't bother to answer. Instead, a gunshot rings out from behind us.

I spin around just in time to see Jorge gripping his chest, stumbling backward as blood spills from between his fingers. He crumples to the ground, gasping.

"Jorge," I start to move toward him, but Shephard blocks me, shoving a gun in my face. His eyes gleam with twisted satisfaction.

"Nuh-uh. Not so fast."

"Shephard?" I growl, fury building in my gut. "What the fuck are you doing?" My gaze flicks between him and Jorge, who's now bleeding out on the pavement.

Shephard's grin is sickening. "Well, let me tell you a little story. Thirty years ago, I had a thing for a cute blonde. She turned me down for *him*." He jerks his gun toward Brickton. "Loyalty's a bitch, right? So I stayed like a good dog until I couldn't anymore. When I offered her an out from her marriage, she told me to get lost." His grin widens as Brickton's face goes pale.

Brickton's hand twitches for his gun, but Shephard's aim never wavers. Our men are already being disarmed by the red-headed guy's crew. We're surrounded, trapped.

Shephard continues, voice dripping with mockery. "So, I took the bitch's life myself when she wouldn't take it. Made you all believe it was a hit from some random club in Ohio. Funny thing is, they actually exist. Well, they did until a few minutes ago."

Brickton's voice is low and shaking with controlled fury. "Did we kill innocent men, Shephard?"

"Innocent?" Shephard laughs, a cruel sound. "No. They were involved in their own shady shit. Trafficking, drugs, you name it. So yeah, you did the world a favor. I had my own reasons for leading you there."

The betrayal sits heavy, twisting like a knife in my gut. I glance at Brickton. He's barely holding it together, his whole body trembling with rage.

"What now?" I ask, locking eyes with Shephard, my voice a dangerous growl.

He sneers. "Now? Well, I hear daughters are even wilder than their mothers. With the cameras I had planted in Nicole's house, let's just say you two put on quite the show last night." His grin turns depraved. "You've got a real dirty mouth, Maddox. If she likes that, well, she's going to love what my extra twenty years of experience can teach her."

Red. Everything turns to red.

Jorge is no longer moving, most likely dead or on the brink of it. If Shephard has his way, he's going after Nicole. If she refuses him, he'll kill her like he killed her mother. If she doesn't refuse... I can't let that happen. I won't.

I feel Brickton shaking beside me. His hand flexes, reaching for his gun, but it's pointless. Shephard's men have us surrounded. The red headed bastard signals his crew, and guns are raised, aimed at us and our men who are lined up for an execution.

"On one," Shephard says, and I grit my teeth as the countdown begins. "Three. Two. One—"

A single gunshot rings out, but it's not what I expected. I look up just in time to see Shephard's head snap back, a new hole blown through his skull. His body hits the ground with a sickening thud, now lifeless.

For a moment, everything's still, like the world's holding its breath.

Brickton starts laughing, and soon enough, the red headed man and his crew join in. The entire scene feels surreal, as if the tension and chaos from moments ago had never existed. Men, who were just pointing guns at the others, are now helping my guys back to their feet from where they kneel. The whiplash from the twists and turns of the past couple of weeks hits me like a sledgehammer.

"What the fuck is happening?" I demand, still on edge, my voice sharp.

Brickton turns to me, his face softening with relief as he explains it all. "Shephard was the puppet master, Maddox. I found out he was behind everything. Martha's death, the lies, everything that's torn our clubs apart. I couldn't let him know I was onto him. He had bugs everywhere, so I had to play along. You and Nicole? I kept you in the dark for your own safety."

He goes on, describing how he hired someone to leave just enough of a trail to make Shephard paranoid, forcing his hand. Roderick, the red head with the terrible bowl cut, had been working for Brickton all along, feeding Shephard just enough information to lead him to believe he could finally take us both out. All the while, Roderick had been reporting everything back to Brickton. Not even Brickton's own men knew about the plan, keeping it watertight.

Today was supposed to be Shephard's victory, but Brickton had ensured it would be his downfall.

As Brickton speaks, I signal to my guys to lift Jorge's limp body and get him into the truck of the other crew. Roderick's guys, along with Geoffrey and some of my men, accompany him to the hospital in hopes that it isn't too late.

I shake my head in disbelief. "A heads up would've been nice, man."

Brickton looks at me, apologetic. "I know. I'm sorry, truly. If Shephard even suspected I was onto him, this could've gone sideways. I couldn't risk tipping him off."

"Is it really over?" I ask, my eyes flicking to Shephard's lifeless body on the ground.

He nods grimly. "Yeah, it's over. Finally."

Relief washes over me, though the adrenaline crash is starting to settle in hard. "This whole thing's giving me a fucking headache," I mutter, rubbing my temples. "I'm getting my girl, taking her home, and I'm sleeping for days." I mount my bike, waving for my men to follow.

When we pull up to the warehouse, I take a moment to thank each of my guys for their loyalty. The weight of the day lingers, but for the first time in what feels like forever, there's a sense of closure.

As I turn towards the warehouse doors, Nicole comes running out, her face lighting up as she leaps into my arms, her legs wrapping tightly around my waist. Her lips crash into mine with a mix of desperation and relief.

"Well?" she breathes against my mouth, her eyes searching mine.

I grin, brushing her hair back from her face. "I'll let your dad explain the details but it's over."

"Good." She presses another kiss to my lips, her voice soft as she says, "Take me home, Maddox."

We mount my bike, and for the first time in months, I feel the kind of peace I've been craving. The ride home is slow, leisurely, the wind whipping through my hair as Nicole clings to me tightly, her warmth grounding me.

Three days later, I am moved back into the house we bought together. The place that was once just a past memory now feels alive again, filled with her presence and mine. It feels right. It feels like home.

Nicole is my world, always has been, and losing her for that year was pure hell. Now that she's back in my arms, I make a promise to myself, no more control. After her mom passed, I gripped too tight, but I won't make that mistake again.

Nicole's already landed a job at a new gentleman's club that opened in town. She loves the freedom, the dancing, and I make damn sure the owner knows exactly who I am and what will happen if anyone tries to push her into doing something she doesn't want.

She sticks to dancing, and I'll admit, I love watching her. Men in the crowd whistle, eyes following her every move, but I know the truth.

They only see a fraction of who she is. Only I know how good she feels off that stage, wrapped up in my arms, where she's always meant to be.

Five months have passed since that chaotic day and today marks Jorge's return to the shop for the first time since he was shot. As soon as he walks into the bay, the place erupts with cheers and whistles, men pounding their fists in celebration. He grins wide, lifting his arms as if soaking in the love from the crew. It's impossible not to join in, the sense of family among us tighter than ever after everything that went down.

Jorge is a tough bastard, surviving a point-blank shot, and seeing him back in action makes everything feel like it's falling into place again. He crosses the room, and I meet him halfway, gripping his hand and pulling him into a hug, clapping him on the shoulder.

"Good to have you back, brother," I say, looking him over with a grin. "About time you stopped laying around."

He laughs, rubbing his chest where the scar peeks out from his collar. "Ain't that the truth."

The last five months have been incredible. Nicole and I have been fucking like rabbits every day, making up for lost time. I'm not even trying to slow it down. If anything, I'm ready to make sure this keeps going forever. She's been happier than I've ever seen her, truly happy for the first time since her mother was killed. There's a light in her eyes that was missing for a long time, and seeing it makes me fall for her even harder.

The betrayal by Shephard, someone she'd known and trusted all her life, was a tough pill to swallow. She's stronger than anyone gives her credit for. She bounced back with a resilience that floors me every day. Between me and her father, she's got the support she needs, and she knows she's never alone in this.

I've scaled back the vigilante work for a while, keeping things low key for now. The guys and I haven't had any major operations since we took down Shephard, but I know it's only a matter of time before we get wind of some more trouble brewing. There are always bad guys out there, always something to set right. For now, I'm enjoying the calm. I'm soaking in the quiet moments, the simple life of loving Nicole and coming home to her every day.

The idea of forever with her has been gnawing at me for weeks now. I love this woman more than I could ever put into words. She's my world and losing her once taught me how fragile everything is. I'm not letting that happen again.

So, this weekend? I'm making it official. I've already bought the ring. A simple, elegant piece that suits her perfectly. Nothing flashy, because that's not her style. But it's solid, just like we are. The plan is to propose this Saturday, make her mine indefinitely.

I can already picture it, the surprise in her eyes, that radiant smile spreading across her face, the way she'll probably try to act all tough, but I know she'll be crying before I even get the words out. After that? We'll keep doing what we've been doing, building a life, loving each other, and never looking back.

Jorge slaps me on the back, pulling me out of my thoughts. "You still in there, man? You look like you're a million miles away."

I chuckle and shake my head, leaning against the workbench. "Just thinking about the weekend."

"You and Nicole got plans?"

I nod, a sly grin spreading across my face. "Yeah, big ones."

Jorge catches on immediately, his eyes widening. "No shit? You're finally doing it?"

"Yep. This Saturday." I pull out the ring from my pocket and show him. His jaw drops.

"Damn, Maddox. That's... man, she's going to flip."

I chuckle, slipping the ring back into my pocket. "Yeah, I know. But in a good way."

The rest of the guys are still celebrating Jorge's return, the noise around us growing louder. For me, all I can think about is Nicole. The weekend can't come fast enough. Soon, she'll be mine forever.

That's the only thing that matters now.

Chapter 12

Nicole

I wake up to an empty bed, but Maddox's side is still warm, leaving a lingering sense of his presence. It's comforting and disorienting all at once. I take a slow breath, my fingers brushing over the crumpled sheets, and then I slip into my robe, tying it snugly around my waist. The house is quiet, the kind of silence that feels almost heavy, as though it's holding its breath for something. I pad softly down the hallway, the faint scent of Maddox's cologne guiding me to the kitchen.

When I enter, I find him leaning against the counter, his broad shoulders tense, eyes distant as he stares out the window. The early morning light casts a soft glow on him, making him look almost ethereal, like a figure carved out of shadows and sunlight. For a second, I just stand there, watching him, feeling a warmth curl inside my chest.

"Good morning," I finally say, walking over and slipping my arms around his waist, pressing my cheek against his back.

He startles under my touch. Maddox, the man who never gets caught off guard. That momentary flinch sends a ripple of unease through me. I can feel the tension in his muscles coiled tight, and the way he hesitates before covering my hands with his own.

"You okay, Maddox?" I ask, trying to keep my voice light, but I can't mask the concern creeping in.

He turns around, his face softening as he looks down at me. There's something in his eyes. A mix of affection and something deeper and darker. Before I can dwell on it, he pulls me into a hug, kissing my forehead, and for a brief second, everything feels right again.

"I'm great," he says, but his voice betrays him. There's a slight hesitation, a crack in the usual confidence he carries. "What do you say we go for a walk through the park this morning?"

I smile up at him, though my heart feels a little heavy. "Sure, that sounds nice."

Even as I say the words, I can't shake the feeling that something is off. I want to press him, to ask what's really on his mind, but instead, I let it go. We grab a quick breakfast at the little shop down the street, our usual spot, before Maddox pulls up to a large park. The autumn air is crisp, filling my lungs with its cool embrace as we hop off his bike. He takes my hand, fingers threading through mine, but his grip is tighter than usual, as if he's holding on just a bit too hard.

The park is beautiful, the leaves tinged with hues of orange and gold, a perfect canvas of fall splendor. We walk in comfortable silence, following the path toward the pond. The pond itself shimmers under the soft morning sun, the surface rippling as geese and ducks glide lazily across the water. Ahead, the little white bridge stretches over the pond, its railing covered in vines with flowers blooming in shades of pink and lavender.

We stop in the middle of the bridge, the peacefulness around us only amplifying the beating of my heart. I take in the scene, the gentle splash of water from the fountain in the center of the pond, the light breeze teasing the edges of my jacket, the way Maddox stands beside me, silent and still. It's the perfect moment, and my own secret presses against my chest, eager to break free.

I draw in a deep breath, turning to face him, but when I do, he's no longer standing. My eyes widen, my breath catching in my throat as I see him kneeling in front of me, one knee bent, a small silver box in his hand. Time seems to slow as he opens it, revealing a diamond ring that catches the sunlight and sparkles like a promise.

My hands fly to my mouth, my heart pounding so loudly I'm sure he can hear it.

"Nicole," he begins, his voice steady yet thick with emotion. "I've loved you for over a decade. I loved you when I was just the son of the Wolves' leader, and even more when I took over after his death. You stood by me, even when I didn't deserve it. Even though I pushed you away, my love for you never wavered."

His words hit me like a wave; every memory we've shared flashing through my mind. The laughter, the fights, the moments of quiet understanding. All of it.

"Nicole Erin," he continues, his voice softening, "will you let me keep proving to you how much I love you, how much having you back in my life means to me? Marry me, Nicole. Please."

Tears blur my vision, my emotions swirling in a chaotic whirl inside me. I can't speak. I can only nod quickly until I'm dizzy from it. Maddox's eyes soften with relief as he slips the ring onto my trembling finger, his lips brushing my skin with a tenderness that makes my heart ache.

He stands and pulls me into his arms, the strength of his embrace grounding me as I clutch his shirt, holding him as if I'll never let go. He leans down, his lips finding mine in a kiss that's both sweet and intense, filled with the weight of everything we've been through.

"I love you, future Mrs. Braise," he murmurs against my lips, his voice husky with emotion.

"I love you too, Maddox," I whisper, feeling the weight of the moment settle in my chest, warm and solid. "My big, bad, fearless MC leader."

As we stand there, the world around us seems to fade away, leaving just the two of us. Two hearts ready to be bound together, stronger than ever.

As I stare into his eyes, still caught up in the warmth of our shared moment, the truth presses at my chest, desperate to be spoken. My heart hammers against my ribcage, and I know I can't wait any longer. Maddox deserves to know everything, he deserves to know this next piece of our life together.

I swallow hard, trying to gather the courage as my fingers fidget on his arms. "Maddox," I start softly, my voice barely above a whisper. His eyes remain locked on mine, soft but curious, like he can sense there's more to come. "I have something I need to tell you."

His brows draw together slightly, just enough to show concern, but he doesn't lose that smile. His lips still curve, radiating the happiness of the moment. I feel my pulse quicken as I reach into the pocket of my jeans, my fingers brushing against the small, folded square that has been burning a hole in my pocket since the doctor handed it to me.

With trembling hands, I pull it out and carefully unfold it, revealing the grainy black-and-white image that has already changed my life in more ways than I can explain. The ultrasound. Our future. I hold it up for him, my hand shaking just slightly as I offer him this glimpse of what's to come.

He takes a moment to look at it, his eyes scanning the picture. His breath catches, and his smile grows wider, broader, until it's stretching across his entire face. "Really?" he asks, his voice thick with emotion, a slight glint of unshed tears gathering in his throat. His eyes glisten, but they never leave mine. In this moment, he is completely vulnerable. A side of him so few get to see.

"Yes," I breathe out, finally releasing the weight I'd been holding inside. "I'm due roughly in April."

The words hang in the air for a beat, and then, like a spring being released, Maddox lets out a loud, joyful holler that echoes across the park. It startles a few people nearby, their heads turning in our direction, but I don't care. He scoops me up in one swift motion, spinning me around with so much force that I lose my breath, a mixture of laughter and tears escaping me all at once. My jacket flutters around us like wings as we spin, Maddox's excitement contagious, lifting me up into the sky with him.

People walking past us on the bridge glance over with smiles, some stopping briefly to watch, but the world around us fades into a blur of colors and motion. The only thing that exists is us. Me and Maddox and this incredible, overwhelming love that's wrapping itself around us.

When he finally sets me back down on my feet, he's breathing heavily, his chest rising and falling rapidly as if he's run a marathon. My hands grip his arms, steadying myself as though I might float away. His dark eyes search mine, glowing with an intensity that makes my heart race all over again. In this moment, I can see the future we're going to build together, the family we're going to be.

"I can't wait to be a family with you," he says, his voice a soft rumble, filled with awe and wonder. His gaze lowers briefly to my stomach, still flat, still unchanged, but it's as if he can already picture the life growing there, the tiny heartbeat that will soon become a part of us.

I place my hand over his, resting on my belly, and feel the tears welling up again. The idea of being a family with Maddox, of raising a child together, it's overwhelming in the best possible way. He's always been a strong partner, but seeing him like this, so open and emotional, makes me fall in love with him all over again.

"I can't believe it," he whispers, his voice filled with reverence as he leans down, pressing his lips gently to my forehead. "You've just given me everything I didn't even know I wanted."

Tears slip from the corners of my eyes as I look up at him, feeling an immense sense of peace settle over me. "We're going to be parents, Maddox," I say, the words feeling surreal even as I speak them aloud.

He cups my face in his large, warm hands, brushing away my tears with his thumbs, his expression soft and full of love. "Our baby's going to be one lucky kid, having you as their mother," he murmurs, his voice tender, a deep contrast to the rough edges that usually define him.

I smile through my tears, wrapping my arms around his neck and pulling him down for a kiss. It's slow, lingering, filled with the promise of everything we're about to experience together. When we finally pull apart, we stand in silence for a few moments, just holding each other, letting the weight of this new chapter sink in.

The park hums with life around us, the distant sound of laughter, the rustling of leaves, the soft ripple of the pond, but all I can focus on is the man holding me close, the man who's about to be the father of my child.

As we start walking again, hand in hand, toward the exit of the park, I glance up at him and catch him staring at me with a smile that reaches his eyes. "What?" I ask, feeling self-conscious under his gaze.

He chuckles, shaking his head. "I'm just trying to wrap my head around it all," he says, his thumb brushing over my knuckles. "Everything's changing, and yet it feels like it's exactly how it's supposed to be."

I lean into his side, my heart full to the brim. "Yeah," I whisper, feeling the truth of his words resonate deep inside me. "It's perfect."

As we leave the park, the future stretches out before us, bright and wide and filled with endless possibilities. Our story is only just beginning, and for the first time in a long time, I can't wait to see what comes next.

From The Author

Dear Reader,

Thank you from the bottom of my heart for taking the time to read my story. I poured so much into these pages, and knowing you've shared this journey with me means the world. Your support fuels my passion for storytelling, and I hope this book brought you excitement, joy, or even a much-needed escape.

If you enjoyed the story, I'd love to hear your thoughts! Reviews are incredibly valuable, not just for me as a writer, but also for fellow readers looking for their next adventure. Whether it's a few words or a detailed review, your feedback makes a difference.

Thank you again for being part of this journey. Until next time, happy reading!

With gratitude,

Tasia Timm

Authors Work

Binding Hearts Series:

Binding Hearts: Book One

Binding Hearts: Book Two

Where Do I Belong

Bound By Love

Flesh & Flame Series:

Flesh & Flame

**Ruin & Rage

**TITLE TBA

The Avenging Angels Series:

Crimson Knights

Zaffre Wolves

The Fake Date

Second Chance Romance Series:

His to Rescue

**Pieces of Us

**To Be Released

Made in United States
North Haven, CT
12 February 2026

88590864R00095